THE BACKSTAGERS

AND THE GHOST LIGHT

BOOK ONE

BY ANDY MIENTUS

ILLUSTRATED BY RIAN SYGH

BASED ON THE BACKSTAGERS COMICS
CREATED BY JAMES TYNION IV & RIAN SYGH

AMULET BOOKS

NEW YORK

LIBRARY OF CONGRESS CATALOGING-IN-PUBLICATION DATA

NAMES: MIENTUS, ANDY, AUTHOR. | SYGH, RIAN, ILLUSTRATOR.

TITLE: THE BACKSTAGERS AND THE GHOST LIGHT / BY ANDY MIENTUS; ILLUSTRATED BY RIAN SYGH.

DESCRIPTION: NEW YORK: AMULET BOOKS, 2018. | SERIES: THE BACKSTAGERS; 1 | SUMMARY: WHEN JORY TRANSFERS TO ST. GENESIUS PREP, HE JOINS THE STAGE CREW AND DISCOVERS THE MAGIC THAT HAPPENS BACKSTAGE BUT WHEN SOME CAST MEMBERS PLAY WITH A SPIRIT BOARD, THE GHOST LIGHT GOES OUT AND STRANGE THINGS BEGIN TO HAPPEN.

IDENTIFIERS: LCCN 2018014306 | ISBN 978-1-4197-3120-4 (HARDBACK)

SUBJECTS: | CYAC: THEATER—FICTION. | CLUBS—FICTION. | MAGIC—FICTION. | SUPERNATURAL—FICTION. | HIGH SCHOOLS—FICTION. | SCHOOLS—FICTION. |

BISAC: JUVENILE FICTION / PERFORMING ARTS / THEATER. / JUVENILE FICTION / ACTION & ADVENTURE / GENERAL. / JUVENILE FICTION / SOCIAL ISSUES / FRIENDSHIP.

CLASSIFICATION: LCC PZ7.1.M519 BAC 2018 | DDC [FIC]—DC23

PRINTED AND BOUND IN U.S.A.
10 9 8 7 6 5 4 3 2 1

ABRAMS The Art of Books
195 Broadway, New York, NY 10007
abramsbooks.com

FOR MY DAD, BOB,
MY MOM, JEANIE,
MY BROTHER, JOE,
AND MY HUSBAND, MICHAEL,
WHO ARE BEHIND THE SCENES
OF EVERYTHING I DO, AND
FOR ALL THE GHOSTS
OF THE THEATER

CHAPTER 1

THERE ARE A LOT OF MYTHS SURROUNDING THE THEATER—COUNTLESS TALES of doomed productions miraculously coming together just in time for opening night, of pants split right in the middle of big solos, of romances blossoming backstage on a ten-minute break and lasting for life.

Of course, most of these stories have little resemblance to the events that actually took place—theater kids have a way of embellishing their stories as much as they embellish their lockers with *Playbill*s and show posters—but then, no one becomes a theater kid to look at life the way it *actually* is.

One theater myth that is particularly pesky is that the kids standing in the spotlight—the Onstagers—have all the fun and all the power, while the kids who control those very spotlights are just working in service of making the Onstagers shine. Which is so far from the truth!

Imagine if one of those Onstagers did something to tick off the wrong Backstager. That spotlight might just *happen* to malfunction during the Onstager's big solo and plunge that kid's shining moment into literal darkness.

Anyone who believes that particular myth has obviously never felt the power of illuminating someone else's biggest moment with the touch of a button, and they have definitely never felt the joy of getting to wear a radio headset during a closing night performance, barking out cues and commands like a starship captain about to enter hyperdrive.

"Sasha, I HEARD that all the way in the light booth!" Beckett brayed into his headset, trying to sound stern but also trying to keep Diet Coke from spraying from his nose through his laughter. "That" which he heard all the way from the light booth was a big booming belch that erupted from the wings, interrupting a very tender and intimate moment of *Lease*, the tragic rock opera that was playing its final performance at St. Genesius Preparatory High School.

"How did you know it was me!?" Sasha asked. Ironically, the bellowing burp came from the smallest Backstager of the bunch. Sasha's mop of blond hair appeared before he did, followed by his round, rosy face, tilting up with a big smile.

"Come on, dude, we all saw you housing that burrito on dinner break," Beckett said. With his green spiky hair, plugs in his earlobes, and thick black glasses reflecting the constellation of light board controls below him, Beckett looked like a live wire and was fittingly high-strung in most situations. It didn't help that he was never without a steady drip of caffeine from the cans and cans of Diet Coke he drank daily. When you power the lighting AND sound of a major theatrical production, something has to power *you*. Tonight, though, with all of the electrics work on the production almost behind him, he was relaxed and enjoying himself.

"Guys, focus, we're moving into the finale. All hands on deck!" That was Hunter, official head builder of the St. Genesius Backstagers and unofficial leader of the group. He was a big bear hug of a guy whose tall brown hair added at least a half a foot more to his already impressive frame. He shot an eye roll across the stage to the opposite wing, where Jory, the newest Backstager (and Hunter's newest boyfriend), was stationed.

Jory was smiling like an idiot. There is a special kind of warm feeling you get from managing to sneak a private moment in a crowded theater, and it is extra special when that private moment is part of a blossoming romance. Averagely tall, averagely built, averagely smart, and averagely social, Jory couldn't believe that someone as remarkably, unbelievably, write-in-your-journal-about-it awesome as Hunter had noticed him so quickly in his first year at his new school. In his hometown, before his mom got her new job and they had to move, he always considered himself kind of invisible. Maybe that's why he was so suited to making magic behind the scenes as a Backstager. Here, surrounded by his new friends, excelling in a new role, and finding his groove in a new place so quickly, he didn't feel invisible at all. Tonight he felt incandescent.

"Have they gotten to the part about how they're too artsy to pay their bills? Oh wait, that's been all night . . ." Aziz wasn't much impressed with the message of *Lease*. In fact, Aziz had found most of the shows St. Genesius had produced in his time as a Backstager cheesier than the kind of birthday cards parents give to each other. All that emotion, all that enthusiasm, all that SINGING—it made him cringe a thousand cringes. Still, as much as he hated what was happening onstage, he loved being backstage exponentially more, so he put up with it. Plus, Sasha was his best friend from childhood, and it was his duty to look out for him. Two birds, one glittery, obnoxious, all-singing, all-dancing stone.

"Hey, everybody shut UP," Beckett commanded. "Her song is starting!"

All the Backstagers went quiet on headset, because Bailey Brentwood, a student from the nearby Penitent Angels School for Girls and, without question, the Coolest Girl in the World, was beginning her big number. For every show, St. Genesius brought in one girl from Penitent to play the female lead, and for the last three years, Bailey was cast every time, because she was truly a star. Even Aziz had to marvel at how she could take the most clichéd, classic show tune and make it fresh and personal. Moreover, unlike so many of the other actors who were loud, hyperactive, and generally terrifying to the Backstagers, Bailey could hang.

They also went quiet because they all knew how much Beckett loved watching Bailey sing. Beckett and Bailey had become close friends freshman year when he was a student at Penitent Angels. Beckett transferred to Genesius before this, his sophomore year, and now he only got to hang with Bailey during the runs of the shows. He missed her a lot. The guys also knew that Beckett had a big, fat, teen-movie crush on Bailey, but he didn't *know* that they knew and so they let him go on thinking that he was smooth about it.

Bailey had an inner glow about her, but she also had an outer glow with her impossibly sleek and shiny long dark hair and skin that was almost literally golden. As she began her plaintive solo, "Today Is Our Only Day," you could hear a fly's heartbeat, the audience was so still. Sasha was feeling very relieved that he'd let one rip when he did, because if any gas escaped him now, Beckett would surely place an eternal curse on him and his entire family. It was shocking, then, when Beckett broke her spell, speaking low and urgently over the radio.

"Backstagers. We have a *problem*."

In an intense whisper, Beckett told them that Bailey's mic was reading low battery. He would go fix it himself when she came offstage next, but the upcoming lighting sequence was too tricky for autopilot. Someone else would have to go backstage to get her a new battery from the sound room.

"I'm doing Kevin McQueen's quick change," Aziz said. "If I miss that, we all know he'll have me arrested for theatrical assassination."

"Yeah, and I have to do the scene change back to the gigantic artist's loft," Jory said. "For starving artists, their open-concept floor plan is really impressive."

"I'll do it!" Sasha exclaimed. "I shall be the savior of mic packs, and children will speak of my noble deeds!"

"Um, Sasha, don't you have *major* props business to attend to?" Aziz asked, an edge in his voice.

"Nope! I'm free for, like, four scenes!"

"Sasha, are you *sure*?"

"Sure, I'm sure!"

"Because I thought we *talked* about how *busy* you'd be at this part . . ."

"Aziz, you KNOW this is my built-in pee break! We all remember what happened during *Les Terribles* when I didn't have—"

Aziz cleared his throat loudly over the radio.

"Oh!" Sasha blurted. "RIGHT, yes, I'm—there's a prop EMERGENCY! With—glue! I've sat in glue and now my butt is glued to . . . all the props. And I can't move. So. Dealing with that. Right now. And—"

"Okay, guys," Hunter interrupted. "I got this."

It was just as well, because Hunter was a junior and had the most experience in the backstage. All of the guys were talented and dependable, but if you wanted something done fast, Hunter was your man.

For such a big guy, he moved like a ninja in the wings, his black crew clothes blending in with the hanging black curtains as he deftly made his way to the back wall of the theater, where he descended a staircase, deeper into the dark. At the bottom of the stairs, past some set pieces left over from their recent, acclaimed production of *Les Terribles*, he reached the stage door, which was unremarkable save for the thick padlock holding it shut. He pulled a key ring off the back of his tool belt, pressed the key into the lock, and paused for a moment.

He hadn't been in the backstage for weeks. After everything that went down during the rehearsal period of *Lease*, the Backstagers had decided to padlock the door and to only go back there for extreme theatrical emergencies, at least until they had a new faculty advisor. Their last advisor, Mr. Rample, was fired in the wake of the incident, and while they all felt reasonably comfortable backstage by now, no one knew it like Rample. If anything unexpected went down without him, they'd be on their own.

Just past the stage door, Hunter walked into the Backstagers' Club Room, and his heart sank a little. The Club Room was their own personal nerd-cave. There were no teachers there, no parents, and best of all, NO actors. Instead, there was a ratty old red couch, a much-loved gaming console and TV, a giant stone head from a past production of *Once Upon Some Island*, and a million stories. The names of every Backstager who had ever crewed at Genesius were graffitied on the brick wall that surrounded the stage door, and artifacts from all those boys' time in the backstage filled the Club Room with a history you could feel. No one knew how the hatchet got buried into the wall above the couch, or even what show needed a REAL HATCHET, but one of the names spray-painted on the wall knew, and so they left it as a sign of respect and in hopes that whatever legends they left behind after graduation would be protected and preserved.

Hunter had missed this place. Starting tomorrow, after the sets and props and costumes were struck and stored, the Backstagers would enter the downtime between productions, when they spent time in the Club Room without any set building or light hanging to interrupt their chillaxation. Maybe they could talk about removing the lock and getting things back to normal. He couldn't imagine downtime anywhere else.

But now was not the time to think about tomorrow, for "Today Is Our Only Day" (gosh, he couldn't get that SONG out of his HEAD!). He walked to another padlocked door, this one of heavy metal and marked UNSAFE. He twisted the key, opened the door, and stepped through it into the darkness beyond.

Now he was in the tunnels—a seemingly endless sprawl of twisting and turning paths lined by innumerable unmarked doors and lit only by a sea of stars hanging impossibly high overhead.

Which brings us to the greatest theater myth of all.

CHAPTER 2

YOU KNOW THAT THING WHEN YOU SEE A SHOW AND YOU KNOW YOU are looking at a room that is missing a wall, you can see the wires making the kids fly, it's obvious that the maid is pouring air into the ladies' cups instead of tea, and people start spontaneously breaking into song in the middle of conversation—but for some reason, you just go with it, and by the end you're leaping to your feet and slapping your hands together?

That's the magic at the heart of theater. All the Backstagers really knew about the tunnels and what lay beyond them is that they were a connection directly to that magic. When Jory joined the team earlier that year, he had a million questions about how it all worked—did they enter a different dimension in the backstage? How many rooms were there in total? What did the fantastical creatures that lived back there eat? How has it all gone unnoticed by scientists and stuff for all this time? The Backstagers didn't know the answers to any of this.

Here's what they did know.

WHAT WE DO KNOW (A WORKING LIST FOR ST. GENESIUS BACKSTAGERS ONLY)

1. The tunnels lead to the rooms.
2. Each department has its own room—a sound room, a prop room, a lighting room, and so on.
3. There are also rooms for, like, tigers and stuff. These rooms are weird.
4. The tunnels change when they feel like it, so the path to any specific room is never the same twice.
5. However, the ORDER of the rooms remains the same. Memorize the order and you should be able to find your way around.
6. The tunnels connect the St. Genesius stage to all of the other stages in the world. If you go too far, you may end up in another school, another state, or another country. You may also run into girls. Proceed with caution and don't smell bad.
7. Time is funky in the backstage. You might go in for a couple of hours and come out to learn you have been missing for weeks. Keep it short.
8. If you reach the Patchwork Catwalk, TURN BACK.
9. So far, we have found no bathrooms in the backstage. Pee first.

As Hunter made his way through the tunnels, he felt a familiar surge of excitement and adventure. He opened a door at random to see where he was. Behind it was a river of color, like an oil spill, cascading in every imaginable shade at once down a craggy mountain through pools and waterfalls. The paint room. He was close.

He counted one, two, three, four doors to the left and swung the door open. He was greeted by several thousand squirrels in top hats right in the middle of a lavish squirrel musical number. Their squirrel musical instruments squealed to a halt, and they all turned to look at him. He stared. They stared right back. He apologized and shut the door gently.

After retracing his steps and counting again to the right this time, he found the correct door.

The sound room looked like a Roman temple, except instead of columns, the ornate ceiling was held up by giant speakers all pointing toward the center. Rainbow-y streams of visible sound flew overhead. If one zoomed close enough to you, you would hear a snippet of some theater's production from somewhere in the world. Songs from *Hey There Molly* and *His Majesty and Me* blended in midair with a scene from a Greek tragedy IN Greek and a symphonic movement, creating a cacophony. Hunter snapped open a compartment on his tool belt, retrieved a pair of orange earplugs, and blocked out the noise so he could focus.

He scanned the stone floor. Every few tiles, there was a handle labeled with a strange series of hieroglyphs—letters that didn't seem to belong to any language currently used on Earth. Luckily, in Hunter's three years of Backstager experience, he knew which one meant "batteries." He located the correct handle and pulled it upward. A whole shelving unit rose easily out of the floor, extending just above Hunter's towering height—hair included.

The shelves of the unit were lined neatly with pristine, fully charged battery packs. Once he located the proper one, he pushed lightly on one of the shelves, sending the unit smoothly back into the floor, and gasped, for when the shelving unit disappeared, he could see two faceless figures in long black robes standing silently across the room, looking right at him. One was tall and quite thin and the other shorter and more solid. They both stood motionless, as if they were totems erected in this temple eons ago, but Hunter had been in the sound room many times and knew that these figures most definitely didn't belong here.

"Who—who are you? How did you get in here?" Hunter asked, trying to hide the quaver in his voice.

The figures stood silently. Then one of them opened its robe slightly and extended its arm, pointing a bullhorn at

Hunter as if it were a pistol. The figure pulled the trigger, and a blast of visible sound, just like the streams flying overhead, came whizzing straight at Hunter. It hit him in the chest, and while his earplugs muffled the intense blast of sound—something like a freight engine's whistle combined with a lion's roar—the force of it knocked him to the floor. The dark figures started slowly approaching.

Hunter scrambled to his feet. The taller, armed figure raised its bullhorn again for a second blast. Sound waves raced toward Hunter, but this time, thinking fast, Hunter pulled up on one of the handles at his feet, and a rack of wires blocked the shot, dissipating the sound waves into the cavernous space.

As the shelving unit sank back into the floor, Hunter's gaze darted around, searching. There!

He spotted the handle he was looking for and bounded toward it, ducking left and right along the way, narrowly avoiding blast after blast of roaring green sound waves. He reached the handle and pulled up the attached rack just enough to retrieve the thing he needed.

He looked up toward the figures—and he was right in their sights, nowhere to hide.

Up came the bullhorn once more. The figure pulled the trigger and the roar surged out. Hunter flipped a switch on the handheld mic he had pulled from the floor, and just as

the blast reached him, he batted it away with a concentrated beam of sound pouring out of the handle of the mic in a solid blue line like the beamed sword of a hero in a space epic. It made a kind of *schwiiiiing* sound when he swung it. He looked and felt very, very cool. But now was not the time to feel very, very cool.

Sound sword in hand, Hunter lunged toward his mysterious foes. The taller creature fired repeated, rhythmic blasts in Hunter's path, but he swatted them left and right with his sword, not slowing his pace. He reached the creatures and with a deft flick of his blade, he knocked the bullhorn out of their reach. He raised the sound blade to strike.

"SUCCESS!" shouted the disarmed, hooded creature in a suspiciously teenage voice. Hunter stopped in his tracks.

"Duuuuuuude!" hollered the other, shorter creature in a warm, jubilant rumble. "You nailed it! And you looked *so* action hero doing it! I wish I'd gotten a video!"

The creatures took down their hoods, revealing two high school seniors. The taller had long blond hair, angular facial features, and a warm smile. The shorter and rounder had long, thick dark hair. He was just seventeen but had a beard that made all of the male teachers jealous. They were Timothy and Jamie, respectively—the stage managers of St. Genesius. Hunter sighed with relief as he lowered his sword.

"Guys, you scared the crap out of me," he said, panting as the adrenaline wore off and the exhaustion set in.

"I know!" Jamie bellowed. "It was HILARIOUS! Timothy, I told you the hoods would be scarier than the Bigfoot costumes."

"Sorry we had to scare you like that, Hunter," Timothy said. "But it was the only way to really put your skills to the test. And you, my clever friend, have passed! Now the real test can begin."

"Test?" Hunter asked, winded but intrigued.

CHAPTER 3

H E DIIIIIIIID IT, HE DIIIIIIIIIID IT!"

Sasha was running around, singing a little victory song he was improvising on the spot for a blushing but very content Hunter.

The *Lease* cast party was in full swing. As the actors shared tearful farewell hugs, shamelessly flirtatious compliments about one another's performances, and spirited tales of productions long since closed, the Backstagers huddled in a shadowy corner, a safe distance from the terrifyingly chipper actors, warm in the glow of their own private revelry.

The St. Genesius cast parties were always held on the auditorium stage after the sets had been struck and the props and costumes put away into storage. Beckett had thrown together a quick party light cue of colorful pools of light here and there and a few strings of Christmas lights

disguise the less-than-magical atmosphere
A single lightbulb on a metal pole was
he lip of the stage so no one stumbled into
the orchestra pit. Someone set up a little wireless speaker
and streamed Showtune Radio, inviting the actors to sing
along to the tragic, belty ballads and dance along to the
up-tempo showstoppers. A few tables would soon hold
the one magical item that could bring together actors and
Backstagers alike—piping hot pizzas.

"He was BRILLIANT." Timothy grinned. "A sound-
beam sword. Total genius."

"Total stage manager material!" Jamie added as he
mussed Hunter's towering pompadour. (It sprang back into
perfect shape as if by magic.)

"I can't believe you fell for it," Beckett said. "As if I'd let
an actor go onstage without a fully charged mic."

"*Especially* Bailey Brentwood," Aziz quipped, smirking
mischievously. Beckett's red cheeks played against his neon-
green hair like an ugly holiday sweater. Jamie gave Aziz a
private nudge in the ribs and Aziz promptly changed the
subject.

"Where's Jory?"

⋊

Jory was glued to the bathroom mirror, trying to make his
hair look like a person's hair and not a weird sculpture that

a grad school artist would make out of toilet paper rolls. He had just moved to the area a few months ago and had yet to find a barber who could pull off his signature fade. It was little things like this that reminded him that he was still the New Kid, since every other aspect of his life at Genesius had fallen so magically into place. He knew Hunter would think he was cute no matter how bizarre his haircut looked, but still, it wasn't every day you get to give your new boyfriend a triumphant hug after a show well done and a trial well passed, and Jory wanted to show up for that moment looking fresh.

As expected, despite the questionable fade job, Hunter lit up when Jory returned to the group.

"Hey, champ," Jory said. "Sorry we tricked you SO expertly."

"Yeah, you really got me," Hunter said, wrapping him up in a bear hug.

"Lucky me," Jory said, sentimental.

Aziz and Beckett shot each other a squeamish look, but they chose to let the cheesy line fly. It was a cast party, after all.

"Waaaaaait," Sasha cooed, unaware of the Level: Expert flirting going on just feet away from him. "I thought Beckett was training me in lights because he was going to be the next stage manager. Did I blow it for him?!"

"Trials are for upperclassmen only," Timothy said. "Beckett will be assistant stage manager and will have his shot at full status next year."

"And when they are stage managers, can we still hang out, or do I have to call them *sir* and stuff?" Sasha asked.

"You don't call us *sir*, and we hang out all the time," Jamie pointed out.

"This was the qualifying round," Timothy explained. "But the real trial is still ahead. Becoming the next stage manager after we graduate will take everything Hunter has in him. Stage managers have to know every department inside and out."

"And navigate the backstage expertly," Jamie added.

"And know what to do in case anything . . . *unexpected* goes down."

The Backstagers shuddered. When *Lease* was in rehearsal, Jory, Hunter, Beckett, Aziz, and Sasha had gotten trapped in the backstage while a creature called Polaroid tried to erase the walls that separate the backstage from the mundane world. The boys went missing for those two months while they were trapped, resulting in the firing of their faculty advisor, Mr. Rample, and the disbanding of the student Backstagers.

However, one of Genesius's star actors, Kevin McQueen, got roped into the trouble when he wandered backstage, and after the guys rescued him, reuniting him with his twin brother, Blake, and saving the run of *Lease* and possibly the world, the McQueens reinstated the student crew and all was well. All except that Mr. Rample couldn't get his job back. He was the sage of their stage, like a wizard headmaster but with theater magic instead of the regular kind, and he always knew what to do when things got out of hand. Without him, they had decided that it was best to secure the backstage and only go there when absolutely necessary.

Timothy and Jamie were doing their best to lead the group as the stage managers, but even though they were seniors, they were still just teenagers, and there was a lot they didn't know about the backstage. Without Rample, they were as scared as anyone else to go too far back there.

"But for noooooow . . . HE DIIIIIIID IT, HE DIIIIIIIID IT!" Sasha was really feeling his new song, and as he spun and strutted around the circle of Backstagers, he nearly crashed right into Bailey Brentwood, the Coolest Girl in the World.

"Did what?" she asked, catching Sasha by the shoulders just as he was about to topple over from his own excitement. Her long sleek hair was pulled up into a casual ponytail, and even though she was wearing the same *Lease* T-shirt as all the other actors, she had that special Bailey Brentwood glow about her that made it seem like she was always in a spotlight, onstage or off.

"Saved your big number!" Beckett exclaimed, jumping up to meet her. "Yeah, there was a glitch with the mic battery. I checked it before the show, of COURSE, but something funky must have happened, and of course I would have fixed it MYSELF, but I had that big light sequence, so Hunter picked up the slack and got the new battery in time for your song. But I could have done it. Of course—"

"Great work tonight, Bailey," Timothy said, snatching the can of Diet Coke from the over-caffeinated Beckett. "We can't wait to see you again after holiday break for the winter show."

"Thanks, Timothy, but I'm not getting my hopes up. I got the lead in *Lease* and *Les Terribles*."

"AND every other Genesius show for the last three years," Beckett added, a bit too quickly. "You're a shoo-in!"

"Well, I'll do my best," she said, her big squinty smile illuminating the room. She and Beckett were just sort of suspended in their smiling for a moment. Music would have played if they were in a musical and not at a cast party. Jamie, sensing an opportunity, broke the silence.

"Heeeey, the pizzas I ordered should be here any minute. Why don't you two go wait for them out in the lobby?"

"Sure," Bailey said. "I've been wanting some catch-up time with Beckett. You guys seemed SO busy during rehearsals, I felt like you all just disappeared!"

The Backstagers all looked like they just simultaneously farted in an elevator.

"We should go!" Beckett exclaimed, letting them all off the hook. "We don't want that pizza to get cold!"

The Backstagers watched Beckett and Bailey stroll out of the doors of the auditorium like the two leads at the end of an '80s movie.

"I think that's our cue to head out," Timothy said. "We have SAT prep in the morning, and if we stay for pizza, we'll never make it. You boys lock up when everyone is finished, all right?"

"And somebody please talk to Beckett about his game," Jamie said, looking off at Beckett, who had somehow tripped on his way up the aisle but was trying to play it cool in front of Bailey, even though he had obviously skinned his knee.

"He's a sophomore," Timothy replied pityingly. "Give him time."

Jamie laughed and gave Timothy an affectionate kiss on the forehead as they started off. Jory and Hunter shared a beanbag chair, and Jory's wiry frame fit perfectly where

Hunter's was bulky. Beckett and Bailey laughed and glowed all the way out to the lobby.

Aziz scanned all of this and couldn't help but feel a little lonesome. Cast parties were ideal places for flirting, and since the only girl who had ever paid any attention to him ever (a ridiculously lovely Penitent Backstager named Adrienne) was busy with her own strike and her own cast party at her own school, he didn't get to enjoy that particular part of the party.

He looked over to Sasha to see if he was feeling similarly envious, but Sasha was busy trying to lick his own elbow. He thought about middle school, when everyone thought that dating was gross and your friends were just your friends. He hoped that his group pairing off and drifting apart was not an inevitable part of growing up. They were Backstagers, after all, and that was a bond no boyfriend or girlfriend could break. Wasn't it?

Suddenly, there was a shout from the other side of the auditorium.

"NO! No, absolutely not!" Kevin McQueen was in his customary hysterics.

"We cannot invite such energies into this, our temple of the THEATER!" his brother, Blake, agreed.

The McQueen brothers were, without question, the kings of the St. Genesius Drama Club. Their parents provided the funding for the productions (more than respectable by professional standards and absolutely lavish by high school standards) and thus were in charge of choosing, casting, and directing the shows Genesius presented.

However, the elder McQueens were also incredibly busy with business dealings overseas and could not spare the many hours required to produce four full theatrical productions a year. This duty then fell to their twin sons, who just happened to also be perfect for the lead roles in each and every show since they were freshmen. They were actually pretty good onstage, and they definitely cared deeply for the quality of the work, so no one complained too much when they inevitably topped every cast list posted on the auditorium doors.

Once you spent enough time around them, you learned that Kevin had the slightly redder hair, his curls pushed forward, and Blake was blonder with curls tied back, but really they were easiest to tell apart when in costume, playing characters more distinguishable than they could ever hope to be in real life. They were also rarely apart, so usually it was just fine to address them as one singular entity.

Tonight, for instance, they were identically upset over a box that Kevin was holding at arm's length as if he were carrying a trapped mouse by the tail out to the street.

"It's just a game, guys," one of the actors complained.

"Yeah, it'll be fun!" chimed another.

"The ghosts of the THEATER are no game," Blake (or was it Kevin? The lights were dim) replied. The actors crowded around the mysterious box, opening it to reveal an even more mysterious game board.

"Spirit Board. Huh. Where did this even come from?"

"It was under the table there—someone must have brought it."

"Who knows how to use it?"

"I do! You lay the board down, and we all put our hands on this plastic thing."

"It's called a planchette . . ."

"Well, aren't *we* soooo international?"

"Shut up!"

"Guys, focus! We put our hands on the *planchette,* and the ghost guides it to different letters, spelling out a message."

The actors laid out a piece of cardboard with all of the letters of the alphabet, as well as "hello," "goodbye," "yes," and "no," printed on it in a ghostly, old time-y font. They formed a circle around the board, placing their hands on the planchette, awaiting any signs of paranormal correspondence.

"It's not a ghost, it's just us moving it."

"It's a GHOST. You'll see."

"What should we ask it?"

"Ummmmm, if there is a ghost in this theater, did you like the show tonight?"

The actors waited, a rare moment of silence from them.

"Whoa!"

"It's moving!"

"You're moving it."

"No, I am NOT!"

"Well, SOMEONE is moving it."

"It's the GHOST, I'm telling you."

"Everybody shut up—we're getting a message!"

"It's drifting to YES!"

"Oh my gosh!"

"YES! He liked it!"

"Why are we assuming it's a he?"

"It's a boys' school. Why would a lady ghost haunt a boys' school?"

"What should we ask next?"

⋊⋉

The Backstagers shared an eye roll from their corner. The actors were so adorably excitable, but frankly, if you had the attention of a ghost, wouldn't you have more important things to ask it than whether or not it approved of your musical? That's an actor for you.

⋊⋉

"What about, are you a good ghost or an evil ghost?"

"Ooooo, that's good."

"No, that's creepy!"

"YOU said it was just a game—are you scared now?"

"Wait, it's moving again!"

"This was a bad idea."

"Shush!"

"E . . ."

"No! Ah!"

"V . . ."

The McQueens stormed off, tired of the silly game but also thoroughly freaked out.

"I . . ."

"I swear I'm not moving it, are you?"

"L!"

Suddenly, the single lightbulb at the foot of the stage popped dark and everyone, including the Backstagers, screamed at the timing, then fell into roars of laughter.

"It's all right, everyone," Hunter said, wrenching himself from the cuddly beanbag. "Just a blown lightbulb. We'll take care of it."

He turned to the Backstagers.

"There are more bulbs in the Club Room. It's Beckett's department, but we gotta give him his moment with Bailey. Not it!"

"Not it," said Aziz, still looking like he was mulling something over.

"IT!" Sasha exclaimed. The Backstagers looked to him quizzically. "I'm trained in lights, remember? That makes me the second in command!"

"Very true, Sash," Hunter said. "You up to the mission?"

"Sir, yes, SIR!" Sasha shouted, darting clumsily off into the wings.

><

Sasha reached the Club Room and was hit with the same pang of nostalgia that Hunter felt for the place. He wasn't allowed to have video game consoles at home, but the Club Room had a Gamestation 5, and he and Aziz had poured many frenzied hours into Call of Honor together. Gosh, how he missed the battlefield.

He looked at the Gamestation like a cartoon character looks at a pie cooling on a windowsill. Maybe he could put in just five minutes while he was down here. Just a few evil alien soldiers sent back to the mother ship.

He drifted to the coffee table, still cluttered with Backstager artifacts, and picked up the Gamestation controller sheepishly. He held it to his nose and inhaled. It smelled like cheese puffs and victory.

Before he knew it, he was easing back into his well-worn spot on the ratty sofa and powering on the flickering old TV. The Gamestation whooshed on with a satisfying musical tone and the Call of Honor logo glowed from the TV like a cozy fireplace. Sasha's pupils widened in his big round eyes. He was home.

><

Back up on the stage pizza came and was happily devoured, truths and dares were traded, a few quick kisses were stolen, and there was a very clumsy attempt to stumble through a number from last year's winter musical, which went perfectly horribly and came to a breathless, boisterous crash landing when they got to the tap break.

Then it was time for the last hugs goodbye before the winter break. It was just two weeks, but theater kids all bid one another farewell like the father seeing his daughter off to Siberia toward the end of *Violinist on the Ceiling* (spoiler alert).

Hunter walked Jory out to the parking lot, where his mom was waiting in the car.

"Well, have a great couple of weeks," Jory said, trying to sound casual but failing as emotion welled up in his throat. Jory and his mom were driving back to their hometown to spend the holidays with family there, so it would be Jory's first extended time away from his new friends since moving to the town. He was surprised at how emotional it made him.

"You too, Jory. We'll all really miss you," Hunter said. "And I'll really miss you."

Jory threw himself into Hunter's made-for-hugging arms. They embraced for as long as they could, and then Jory was in the passenger seat and St. Genesius was in the rearview mirror. He leaned his head against the window and was quiet.

×

Sasha had very nearly defeated the Spider Queen of Dark Space 12 when he glanced down at his phone and noticed he had five missed calls from the Scrapbooking Queen of Lakeview Drive—his mother.

"Uh-oh," he muttered to no one as he paused the game and called her back, racing out of the Club Room. Sasha's mother had always been a worrier, but since the incident of the Backstagers' disappearance, she was downright inconsolable if Sasha was unreachable for two minutes. It had been fully fifteen. He held the phone an arm's length from his face and could still hear her screaming as he grabbed his coat, shut off the lights in the auditorium, and ran outside.

The empty, dark auditorium was finally still and quiet after weeks of *Lease* performances and the raucous cast party.

A thin wisp of smoke rose from the exploded bulb, still perched dark atop the metal pole at the lip of the stage.

Something else moved in the dark . . . a small, thin shadow slipping past the burnt-out light to the spot where the Spirit Board game still lay abandoned. Two gloved hands lay on the planchette. It began to move.

CHAPTER 4

FOR JORY, BEING BACK IN HIS HOMETOWN WAS A BIT LIKE BEING A GHOST. All of his old haunts still looked and smelled and operated as they always had, but there was something alien about them now. Passing each of these landmarks as he and his mom drove around making holiday visits, he thought about how time and memory seem to put a filter on things the way stage lights do to a set and costumes.

Time put a filter on people, too. A few of his old friends reached out to meet up at the local diner for coffee and pie, and as Jory sat there looking at these faces and hearing these voices he used to know so well, he felt like he was observing them through the wrong end of a telescope. The drama or hilarity of the anecdotes they shared was totally lost on him. Did he really used to care who Becca was sitting with at lunch? Did he really used to quote that meme as much as they all did? Did he really used to crush on Lizzie so hard he turned into a stammering mess around her? Were these people really as close to him as the Backstagers are now, after just a few short months?

All of this swirled in Jory's head and he wasn't sure how to feel about it. On the one hand, he felt infinitely more mature than his old classmates. They were still concerned about Becca, and he and his new friends had literally saved the world just weeks before. He also was certain that he had moved on. He missed his new friends and his new school and couldn't wait to get back. Nothing was tying him to this place anymore. So why did he feel so sad?

Maybe it was this creeping thought—if these places and people that used to mean so much to him left him so cold after such a short time, then all those formative years and experiences were essentially worthless. And who's to say that he won't forget the magic of the backstage and the Backstagers a few months after graduation? Would the rest of his life be like this? Little disposable episodes that play out and then close, leaving him as alone as he was before he started them?

He called Hunter.

"Hey, Jory! Merry Christmas!"

"Merry Christmas to you! How's it going?"

Hunter sighed. "It's fine, trying to balance family stuff with studying for the trials. Do you know what a grommet is?"

"Is that, like, a mythical creature?"

"It's the little metal ring that you hang a curtain by. There is a NAME for that thing. And a million other things. I don't know how I'm gonna learn all this."

"Wow, that's—"

"And did you know there were over five HUNDRED technical cues in *Lease* that Timothy was calling every night? Who can do something perfectly five hundred times in a row? What if you miss one?"

"I'm sure he did miss one or two, it's not really about that—"

"And then the worst part—did you know that the stage managers have to manage the ACTORS?! Like, if any of them has any little problem with the way their shoes fit or if they are running late to rehearsal or their dog dies or something, it's the stage manager's job to handle that? Along WITH the five hundred cues and the grommets and the gels and the spike tape and the gobos and the—"

"Hunter! Slow down, take a breath. You're gonna make yourself crazy."

"Sorry. It's all a bit overwhelming. I mean, I'm a Backstager, but I'm also a junior. I have all of my regular classes to worry about, and I have to start thinking about colleges. I just don't know how I'm gonna get this all done."

"Just take one thing at a time. I'm here for you."

"Thanks, Jory. Yeah. Sorry, I feel like I'm just talking about myself. How are you?"

"Um, well . . ."

Suddenly, Jory's creeping anxiety didn't seem as urgent as when he'd called. Hunter was already stressed enough about *actual* problems; he didn't need to be weighed down further with Jory's fears about *potential* problems. He thought about that *Lease* song, "Today Is Our Only Day." Why worry about stuff that hasn't happened yet? Worry about what is right in front of you.

"I'm great," Jory lied. "I mean, my family is, like, completely exhausting around the holidays, but also adorable, and it is nice to be home."

"I bet. You seeing old friends?"

"Oh yeah, tons. It's been awesome to catch up."

"That's so great, Jory—enjoy it!"

"I will, for sure."

"Well, hey, I could talk to you all night, I really could, but I should get back to this. I only have, like, twenty more minutes of cram time before we have to start family dinner and—"

"No, of course. Do what you gotta do, I'll talk to you tomorrow. Have a great Christmas, Hunter."

"You too, Jory. Big hugs."

"Big hugs."

Jory hung up the phone, and even though he didn't feel less anxious, he felt in control of his anxiety, at least. He had chosen to push it down and rise above it. He suddenly felt very grown up . . . if not exactly better.

CHAPTER 5

JORY COULD FEEL HIMSELF COMING BACK TO LIFE AS HIS MOM'S CAR SPED closer and closer to St. Genesius. He had survived the rest of winter break by entering a kind of hibernation, cooped up in a guest room in his aunt's house consuming a steady stream of junk food and episodes of British baking competition shows.

Not only was he finally returning to the place and the people he loved, but it was an especially excellent time to be a Backstager: downtime, the time between productions of shows. For the next couple of weeks, there would be no sets to build, props to locate, or fires to put out (metaphorical or literal). It was the time some of the best memories were made, and it let the Backstagers recharge a bit before the hard work began on the next show.

When Jory spotted his crew in the cafeteria, he practically pounced on them as they greeted him with the warmth that was so sorely missing from his experience back in his hometown. Now he was truly home.

"JORRRRRRRRRYYYYY," Sasha more sang than shouted. "You missed SO much while you were away! My mom accidentally gave me Christmas cookies with nuts in them and I got a rash that looked like a DRAGON!"

"Truly exciting stuff," Aziz said, patting Sasha on the head affectionately. "Almost as exciting as Sasha's reaction to the allergy medicine."

"I could taste COLORS!" Sasha exclaimed.

"We thought he was a goner for sure," said Aziz, "but he pulled through and his mom felt so bad about the whole thing, she caved and bought him his own Gamestation."

"It was a Christmas MIRACLE! I miss my rash-dragon, though. I named her *Jessica*."

"Anyway," Beckett said, cracking open what must have been his fourth Diet Coke of the morning, "that was the big news around here. That, and my dad learning how to use photo apps on his phone. He thinks he invented the dog-ears filter."

Beckett's phone buzzed in his pocket and he shuddered.

"Ugh. There's another one now. The man has an addiction."

"Where's Hunter?" Jory asked.

"Backstage," Beckett said, replying "LOL" to his dad once again. "He's gonna be taking lunch back there with Timothy and Jamie for a while to do extra trials prep."

"Oh," Jory said, deflating.

"He can't wait to see you, though," Aziz offered. "He talked about you all break."

Jory smiled through his disappointment and they all sat down to lunch.

><

The day crawled toward the final bell, and when it rang, Backstager downtime was ON! Sasha and Aziz went straight for the Gamestation in the Club Room and booted up Call of Honor.

"Okay, Spider Queen," Sasha said, his eyes narrowing, "I've been practicing at home. You shall not survive!"

He and Aziz spent a red-eyed, white-knuckled hour with the game while Jory watched, pretending to be thrilled, really keeping his eye on the Unsafe door that separated him from the backstage and Hunter. Then he got bored and went off to see what Beckett was up to. He found him, per usual, up in the light booth.

"Hey," Jory said, announcing himself. "Whatcha doin'?"

"Trying to untie the Gordian knot of cables the actors left me after the *Lease* strike," Beckett said, clearly agitated. He was crouching in the corner opposite the light board pulling apart long, thick cables like some kind of giant alien pasta. "I told Hunter we shouldn't let them help with strike—it's faster on closing night, sure, but if they put stuff away like this, it takes double the time to set up the next one."

"But it's downtime," Jory said. "Can't that wait until we go back into production?"

"My wires are literally crossed, Jory. I won't sleep until I know everything is put away right."

"Oh, okay. Want some help?"

"Kind of you, dude, I appreciate it, really, but I know where everything goes and I think it'll go faster if I just stay the course."

"Totally. Okay."

Jory started for the door. Beckett sensed his gloom.

"He still not back yet?"

"Not yet, no. And I'm not really much for Call of Honor."

"Ugh, me neither. That's actually how I ended up in electrics—I was so bad at the game, I ended up getting in their way, so I just started hanging out up here. Timothy noticed and trained me on the board. If you wanna hang, Jory, I'd love your help."

"No, Beck, that's okay, I don't wanna get in your way."

"Hopefully I'll be done soon and chillaxing can commence."

"See you then," Jory said as he left the booth.

After checking the Unsafe door one more time for signs of life, Jory made his way to the library. If he got his homework done now, he could be totally free to maximize his time with Hunter and the rest of the guys when they all emerged.

He spread his books out on one of the tables and got to work, but soon his concentration was broken by a group of upperclassmen snickering at the next table over.

"I mean, he wears all black every single day," one of them said. "Like, we get it dude, you're spooky. Someone should tell him to be a little more original."

Jory looked up to see who they were talking about. Across the library, at the most secluded table in the room, a lone boy sat working feverishly on a laptop. He was indeed wearing all black—a slouchy outfit of baggy sweatpants, a long cloak-like sweater, and a big wide-brimmed hat, which made a dark halo around his sleek black hair.

"Who would tell him?" another upperclassman asked. "He doesn't have any friends."

"Careful, don't let him hear you!" said a third. "My buddy Ross got a look at one of his books one day and it was on *magic*. Not like pulling rabbits out of hats, like *spells*. For *real*. He might turn you into a frog!"

Jory's ears pricked up. All-black clothes. Bit of a loner. Interested in magic. Could the boy in the corner be . . . another Backstager?

After the upperclassmen had cleared the room, Jory approached the boy in black. He was standing right over him, but the boy either didn't notice or didn't care. His fingers flew over the keyboard, and his eyes were fixed to the screen. Jory broke the ice—or tried to, at least.

"Hey, sorry to bother you."

No response. Just typing.

"Do you mind if I sit here?"

"Seat's empty," the boy said, not looking up from the screen.

"Cool, thanks."

Jory sat and a full minute passed in silence as the boy worked. Finally Jory just came right out with it.

"So listen, I noticed you were wearing all black and I heard some guys say you knew something about magic and—"

"Okay," the boy said, snapping the laptop shut and looking Jory dead in the eye for the first time. "Let's get this over with. You're here to get a closer look at the witch-kid. Well, here he is. Yes, I'm a witch. No, you don't have to be an old woman with boils on her nose to be a witch. Yes, I do spells. No, I won't do one for you. No, I don't worship the devil—that's a modern, religious invention, so that one is all yours—and no, I don't love that musical with the witches, because frankly I hate all musicals, especially that one, which I find shrill and silly. We done?"

The boy threw his laptop into his shoulder bag (black, of course), and started to scurry off.

"Wait!" Jory said. "I just meant I thought you were a Backstager! I didn't mean to upset you."

"A what?" The boy stopped, frozen between staying and leaving.

"A Backstager. I'm on the crew for the St. Genesius Drama Club. And we tend to wear all black and prefer secluded corners, too. I thought you might be one of us."

"Oh," the boy said, relaxing slightly. "Sorry. I can be a little anxious. Especially around new people."

"I can relate to that for sure. I'm new here at Genesius. I'm Jory."

"Reo. Hey."

"Reo? That's so cool, it's like a name from the future."

"Japanese, on my dad's side. Irish on my mom's, or Celtic, she would say, hence the witch thing. Runs in the family."

"So you're really a witch?"

"Is that weirder than being a *theater* kid?"

"I guess it isn't."

They laughed.

"Those guys back there said you don't have any friends— is that true?" Jory asked.

"Pretty much," Reo said, unashamed. "Most people I've let in tend to get freaked out when I tell them about the witch stuff. I only told one kid I thought was my friend freshman year, and he told everyone, so now the black cat is outta the bag. I decided it's easier not to trust people."

"Is that why you wear black? To scare people away?"

"Black is the color of protection. I wear it as a shield."

"I love that," Jory said. "Well, listen, I totally get it if you do better on your own, believe me, but if you ever get bored of that screen and see me around, feel free to come say hey."

Reo looked touched.

"Okay. Cool. I will."

"See you around, Reo."

"See ya, Jory."

Jory headed back toward the auditorium, feeling a little lighter than before. Then he went almost airborne when he saw Hunter, standing at the end of the hallway, looking for him. Hunter's gaze met Jory's and a smile cracked across his face.

"THERE you are!" Hunter exclaimed as he bounded toward Jory and scooped him up off his feet into a hug. "I am so, so sorry. We were doing quick changes today and I don't know if you gathered this from my *amazing* fashion sense, but wardrobe is really not my department."

"That's okay," Jory said, hugging back tightly. "I understand. I'm just so glad to see you."

For the moment, Jory felt like himself again.

CHAPTER 6

DOWNTIME WAS OVER ALMOST AS QUICKLY AS IT HAD BEGUN. Beckett managed to fix all of the hastily disassembled electrics, but then he found that the sound equipment was left in an equally disastrous state. He ended up spending the entire two weeks cursing under his breath at actors who were more interested in getting to the cast party quickly than properly caring for the things that let the audience *hear* and *see* them.

Sasha and Aziz finally conquered the Spider Queen and Call of Honor and moved on to some medieval role-playing game that had them discussing magic and health stats in a level of detail that would be overwhelming to professional statisticians.

Hunter was almost incessantly preparing for the trials, but he and Jory did manage to hang out a few times. When they did get some time alone, though, Hunter was clearly distracted, no doubt poring over whatever new information had just been thrown at him in his training. Jory didn't blame him—he could tell that Hunter was making an effort, which meant a lot. Still, he couldn't help but be a little disappointed that he spent most of the downtime . . . down.

The Backstagers didn't actually gather all together until the formal end of downtime: the winter term drama club meeting in which the winter musical would be announced.

A meager but enthusiastic crowd of about a dozen boys gathered in the auditorium, whispering rumors and speculation about the official selection and what supporting roles might be available to them. The din of the room reached a crescendo and then suddenly went silent as Kevin and Blake McQueen entered stoically, bearing the full weight of the secret they possessed. They stood at the lip of the stage, gazing out at the deadly still crowd, savoring the drama of the moment.

"Good afternoon, thespians of Genesius," said Kevin. "It is my distinct honor to announce to you the official selection for this year's winter musical."

A dozen simultaneous squeaks rang out as the rapt boys leaned forward in their seats in unison.

"But first, a bit of housekeeping," said Blake. A dozen moans erupted from the boys. Blake smiled, almost imperceptibly. He loved wielding this kind of power over a crowd.

After the McQueens spoke for what seemed like an eternity about mundane things like sign-up sheets, dues, bake sales, and T-shirt orders, Kevin commanded the room with a dramatic, "And NOW . . ."

An underclassman actor wheeled an easel covered by a bit of velvet curtain scrap to the middle of the stage. The McQueens each placed a hand on a corner of the fabric, shared a look and a nod, and pulled the velvet away with a flourish, revealing a poster of a white mask and red rose against an inky black background. In lavish script, it read:

A dozen gasps were followed by a dozen squeals and whispers as the actor boys erupted in frenzied *I told you sos* and *can you believes*.

"Yes," Blake shouted, bringing the crowd back to attention. "We have managed to be one of the first schools in the nation to secure the rights to perform this legendary show. A show that is *still running on Broadway*."

The crowd fell into histrionics again. Kevin continued over the noise.

"For any of you who might have been living under a theatrical *rock*, this is the timeless story of a ghostly composer who haunts a French opera house and falls for its star soprano, the glamorous Crystalline. It will challenge each of us actors with the demands of its operatic score and, indeed, each Backstager as well. For at the climax of the show, the Broadway production features a thrilling effect in which a candelabra shatters and explodes as the Phantasm sings. We will, naturally, be attempting the *very same effect* used on *Broadway*."

A dozen adolescent shrieks pierced the air.

"Auditions will be this Friday here in the auditorium. We will, naturally, be looking to girls from Penitent Angels to find our Crystalline," Blake said, producing a sign-up sheet seemingly from thin air.

Sasha shot Beckett an excited look, but stifled it when Beckett put his face in his hands.

CHAPTER 7

ALL DAY FRIDAY, BECKETT WAS A NERVOUS WRECK. IT WASN'T THE prospect of pulling off the candelabra effect—the only thing Beckett loved more than a challenge was an explosion. No, Beckett was doubling down on the Diet Cokes and cleaning his glasses compulsively every few seconds because he was as nervous for Bailey's audition as if he were auditioning himself.

Bailey was one of the first friends Beckett had made at his old school and one of the only people he still kept in touch with from there. When Beckett knew he needed to transfer from Penitent Angels to St. Genesius, he left the Backstagers at his old school understaffed before the biggest production of the year, and it strained his friendships with most of them. But Bailey met the news with understanding and excitement for him. It meant the world to him and

THE BACKSTAGERS AND THE GHOST LIGHT

cemented Bailey's place in his heart. Beckett always held his breath a bit when Bailey auditioned for the Genesius shows, but he knew that *Phantasm* was her absolute favorite show and Crystalline her dream role. As much as he loved working in the theater, Beckett wasn't much for cast albums of musicals, but no matter how many times Bailey put the *Phantasm* recording on, he pretended to love it because he saw how happy it made her.

Bailey walked into the Genesius auditorium that afternoon with her usual quiet confidence. A row of six other girls fixed their hair and checked their voices as quietly as they could, but Bailey just sat, calmly studying the sheet music for the audition song and sipping lemon tea with honey.

"See, dude, she's got this," Aziz assured Beckett. They were watching way up from the light booth but could feel her poise and determination even from there.

"I know. Right. Like, why should I be freaking out, she's gotten the lead every time. She's a star."

"Right."

"Right. And she has been preparing to play Crystalline all her life."

"Right."

"Right. I mean, she knows these songs like the back of her hand."

"Right."

"Right . . . Right?"

"BECKETT!" Aziz grabbed him by both shoulders. "How many Diet Cokes today?"

"I dunno, the normal amount. Three?"

"Beckett . . ."

"Five . . . FINE. Twelve—only twelve. But I didn't sleep and I need the boost."

"You're going to give yourself a heart condition, my dude. Maybe call it quits for today. And chill out. It's *Bailey*. You said it yourself, she gets the lead every time. This time is no different."

Aziz mussed Beckett's hair, which stood up especially sharply today, and left him alone in the booth. Beckett paced a bit, trying some breath work from a meditation app his mother had made him download, but Beckett was better at taking action than taking breaths. He had a plan.

Crystalline's audition song ended in a famously in-the-rafters high note as she fell under the Phantasm's spell. At that exact moment, Beckett would turn up a warm amber spotlight on Bailey's face with a cool blue light coming from behind her to give her an otherworldly quality. He knew she didn't need it, but it made him feel better to do the one thing he could do to make her shine even brighter.

One by one, the Penitent Angels girls took to the stage to attempt the song, and one by one, they crashed and burned on the final high note. Girl after girl gathered up her things and exited in quiet devastation. Finally, there was just one girl left to audition.

"Brentwood, Bailey," Blake McQueen announced coolly. He, along with Kevin and stage managers Timothy and Jamie, sat behind a long table at the lip of the stage, like judges on a singing competition show, notepads and résumés and pictures of the hopeful actors laid out before them.

Bailey took a moment for herself, drawing a deep breath in and releasing her tension as she exhaled, then stood and made her way to center stage, sheet music in hand. She stood before the table.

"Hello, my name is Bailey Brentwood and I'm auditioning for the role of Crystalline."

She nodded politely to the boy sitting behind the piano in the pit, and he began playing the audition song.

In the booth, Beckett tensed but then immediately relaxed as Bailey began to sing—her voice powerful, her breath confident. She sounded perfect, but she was telling the story of the song so beautifully, you almost didn't notice the technical perfection of the singing. She was acting through song, and it was magic.

Jory watched from his usual spot in the wings and smiled, proud of Bailey. He looked to Hunter's usual spot in the opposite wing to share the moment, but Hunter was gone, so Jory kept the moment to himself.

The climax of the song approached. All of the audition-ing hopeful boys leaned forward in their seats, their eyes glistening with awe at her performance.

Beckett readied his fingers on two slides on the light board. The high note was a few measures away. He slid the controls up, bathing Bailey in amber and blue light. One of the actors watching from the house let out a piercing scream. Bailey stopped singing and turned her head in the direction of the scream just as a huge stage light whizzed past her and crashed violently to the floor.

Beckett watched in horror as the auditorium erupted in screaming and chaos. Timothy bolted up to pull Bailey away from the wreckage. The other actors raced to the foot of the stage to make sure she was okay. Jamie looked up to the light booth.

"BECKETT!" he shouted, uncharacteristically stern. "Production office, now. Everyone else take five."

A group of students took the shaken Bailey to a seat to recover as the stage managers herded the Backstagers to the production office.

"Guys, you know me. I hang all these lights myself and safety is my number one concern," Beckett said.

He was sitting in a chair in the production office, the stage managers standing over him, poker-faced. The other

Backstagers sat at the sides of the room, looking at the floor.

"I tighten them every week and they all have backup cables made of steel. I'm sure of it. I would never let anything like this happen, especially not to—"

Emotion overcame Beckett's voice as he broke down in tears. Timothy put a hand on his shoulder.

"We know that, Beck," he said calmly. "You're the most reliable electrics guy we've ever had. So what is the most rational explanation?"

"I . . . I really don't know," Beckett said, baffled.

"We have to tell the McQueens something, Beckett," Jamie said. "This is on us."

"Well . . . I don't know. I mean, I guess maybe I could have missed one? Somewhere along the way."

Timothy looked to Jamie. They knew as well as Beckett that this wasn't the answer. Hunter stood up.

"This is wrong. Beckett didn't make a mistake. Something funny is going on here, and we all know it."

"Like the bulb shattering," Sasha said.

"Wait, what bulb?" Timothy asked.

"At the cast party," Sasha explained. "We were all using one of those Spirit Boards to talk to a ghost, and that light-bulb that we always leave on exploded."

Jamie looked at Timothy darkly.

"The bulb on the metal pole at the lip of the stage?" he asked.

"Yeah," said Sasha. "But don't worry, I replaced it."

"Right away?" Timothy asked, an urgency rising in his voice.

"Yeah, of course! Oh wait . . . "

"What, Sasha?"

"Well, I went down to replace it right away, but well, I got . . . distracted."

"Sasha . . . " Aziz was frustrated for his friend. He hated seeing him mess up, but it was an all too common occurrence.

"I hadn't been down to the Club Room in weeks and the Gamestation was STARING ME DOWN. I was WEAK! And I just . . . forgot. But I replaced it first thing the next day, I swear!"

"It was dark all night," Jamie said to Timothy, with grave concern.

"Guys," Jory chimed in. "Sorry, but why is this a big deal? What's that lightbulb?"

Beckett raised his face from his hands.

"Every theater in the country leaves one light burning all night," he said. "The Ghost Light. Most would say it's a safety measure to make sure actors don't walk off the lip of the stage and fall into the pit, but it has that name for a reason. It's said to also keep ghosts from moving in."

"Ghosts?" Jory couldn't believe what he was hearing, even knowing all that knew about the backstage.

"Ghosts and theaters are a perfect match," Beckett continued, "sort of like how guys like us are a perfect match for theaters. There are lots of shadowy places to hide, lots of magic all the time. Tons of theaters around the world are haunted, and a lot of the time the ghosts are mischievous but friendly. Given what happened today, though, if something has moved in, I'd say it is decidedly NOT our friend."

Everyone sat in a heavy silence for a moment. Finally Beckett sighed.

"I'll take the fall for the light. Just let me be the one to tell her and apologize. In the meantime, we have to figure out if Genesius really does have a ghost, and if so, what we are going to do about it."

Back in the auditorium, Bailey was shaken but luckily unharmed. The Backstagers filed back in from the wing, and Beckett ran up to where Bailey was recovering.

"Bailey, I don't know what to say. I am so, so sorry."

"I'm—I'm sure it's not your fault."

"But it is. I'm the head electrician. I hang and secure all the lights. It must be my mistake."

"I'm fine. Nobody got hurt."

"I just feel so awful."

"Really, Beckett. I'm okay," Bailey said sharply. Beckett knew it was best to leave it, for now. As much as he wanted to give her a hug, he could tell that she really needed space to gather herself and focus on her audition.

"Okay, everybody," Jamie announced. "We're back from break. We did a spot check of the grid and we feel confident that all of the other lights are properly secured. Thank goodness no one got hurt. Bailey, why don't we try it again, when you're ready?"

"Sure thing," she said, and got back onstage. She didn't get her customary deep breath in before she nodded to the accompanist to begin the song, and though she sounded okay, it was not as powerful as before, and she didn't seem as focused in her storytelling. The high note approached. Bailey tensed up. Her voice faltered and cracked. The piano tinkled to a halt. The room deflated. The McQueens each raised an eyebrow in unison.

"That's okay, Bailey," Timothy said from his seat at the table. "Let's take it again from the bridge."

They started the music again in the middle of the song, and when she reached the final climactic note, her voice again broke in an anticlimactic squeak. Beckett leaped up from his seat in the auditorium, furious.

"Well, of course she's nervous, she almost DIED! Why don't we let her go again another day?"

"ACTUALLY," Blake McQueen shot across the theater, "the legendary role of Crystalline is one that demands an actor's absolute best even on her absolute worst day. This falling light may actually be a test sent from the theater gods to see if this Crystalline is really up to snuff. Would you like one last try, Ms. Brentwood, or shall we see you at auditions for the spring show?"

Bailey steeled herself and nodded to the accompanist again. He began playing, and she attacked the song with verve, fighting for her pride and her shot at her dream role. But all that effort made her clench her throat when the high note came. Once again, she cracked. She looked to Timothy, who looked down at his notepad. Kevin and Blake shared an icy look.

"Thank you," Kevin said. "That's all we need to see today."

Bailey's eyes went glassy but she nodded professionally, descended the stairs at the front of the stage, quickly gathered her things, and made for the exit. Beckett got up and started toward her, but Aziz put a hand on his shoulder.

"Let her have a minute," he said.

"ALAS!" Blake moaned after she had left. "The role of Crystalline is just too demanding for a student to take on! What a catastrophe! How are we going to select another show in this eleventh hour?!"

"Excuse me," chimed a clarion voice from the back of the auditorium. All heads turned to greet the voice.

The girl it came from was equally ethereal. The first thing you noticed about her was long, wavy silver hair, which played against her skin tone like the Milky Way across the summer night sky. Her hair was remarkable not only because of its unusual color, but because it was one futuristic detail on a girl who seemed to walk out of another time. She wore a white lacy short dress, all bows and frills, like she was on her way to a Victorian birthday party. Taking in the hair and the clothes together, you might think about a time you dressed a superhero action figure in a baby doll's dress just to see what you wound up with.

"I'd like to audition," she continued. "Sorry I'm so late. I had talked myself out of coming but then got up the courage. This is my first audition."

"Your first audition ever," Kevin sneered, "is for the role of Crystalline? You do know what a demanding role it is?"

"Where do I stand?" she asked, undaunted. Kevin and Blake looked at each other and gestured to the X on the stage before them. The girl climbed the stairs to the stage,

stood on the X, and waited silently. After a long beat, Blake cleared his throat.

"Um. So. What is your name? Are you ready to begin?"

"Oh yes, of course. My name is Chloe Murphy and I'm ready whenever you are," she said with a simple smile. Kevin stifled a laugh—the poor thing, she had no idea how to do this. Blake nodded to the accompanist, and the music for Crystalline's big song began again.

What happened next was downright spooky.

Chloe began to sing, and the voice that sailed forth from her was otherworldly. It was as technically perfect a soprano as you'd hear on the professional cast recording but shaded with color and feeling none of them had ever heard before. It was the kind of voice that made you hear lyrics you had memorized as if you were hearing them for the first time. She sang the song like she'd written it. As the climactic high note approached, everyone leaned forward in anticipation. Not only did she execute the note effortlessly and flawlessly, but there was something else, too—at the exact moment, two REAL tears rolled gracefully down her cheeks. She had fully embodied Crystalline in all of her pain and longing.

The song ended. No one moved. Blake and Kevin McQueen stared, slack-jawed. Chloe lifted her head and wiped the tears away, returning from Crystalline's world back into hers and regaining her open, wide-eyed expression.

"Is that it?" she asked. "Do I leave now?"

"BRAVA!" Blake erupted. "Brava, Ms. Murphy, and thanks be to the theater gods for sending you!"

"I think we are all in agreement," cheered Kevin, rising from behind the table to shake Chloe's hand.

"We have found our Crystalline!"

CHAPTER 8

HEEEEEEEY, GHOST! HEEEEEEEEEEERE, GHOST!"

Sasha had already covered all of stage left and was nearly halfway through stage right with still no sign of St. Genesius's newest resident—the ghost he had inadvertently let move in.

Sasha was a junior, second oldest in the group just behind Hunter, but was still treated as the kid. This might be because he still found farts hilarious and saw the world through wide-open eyes, but he feared that it might be because he was somehow always getting the Backstagers into messes. The trouble that occurred during the *Lease* rehearsals had been his fault—he had wandered into the backstage and befriended Polaroid, the entity that had attempted to trap them all back there forever and erase the walls that separate the backstage from the outside world. Most kids would agonize in guilt over something like that, but today, Sasha was glad that it had happened—if he had befriended a ghost (or something like a ghost) then, he could do it now, and maybe this one would listen to reason and move out of the theater. Or at least stop dropping lights on people's heads.

When he had finished his sweep of stage right, he sat for a moment in deep thought. His eyes lit up when he got an even better idea, and he raced to the prop closet to gather tools and building materials. He was aware that he had a knack for making messes, but this time, he was determined to be the one to make his mess right.

Meanwhile, onstage, rehearsals for *Phantasm* were in full swing. For the last week, the actors had gathered daily after school to learn the intricate score and begin to stage the scenes and choreograph the dances, while the Backstagers began to design and construct the sets, costumes, props, and effects.

Chloe Murphy had lived up to that promising audition and was becoming the darling of the Genesius Drama Club—a quick study, friendly to everyone, and absolutely incredible in the role. Today, she and Kevin were rehearsing a pivotal scene in the Phantasm's lair where she sings his ghostly opera for the first time. Kevin had won the coin toss and would be playing the Phantasm, while Blake would play Rupert, the young leading man who steals Crystalline's heart and fills the Phantasm with a jealous rage. The Phantasm was the title role, but Rupert had the best song, so there wasn't *too* much family drama over this casting development.

As Chloe and Kevin went through the motions of the scene onstage, Aziz and Jory were huddled in a wing, studying some plans for the big candelabra explosion effect.

"Yeah, I think it's going to work," Jory said, not sounding too convinced.

"The blowing up part, sure," said Aziz, "but then how do we clean it all up in the thirty seconds we have to change to the next scene?"

"Right. Hmm. Maybe we could get the McQueens to move the end of Act One here? Go out with a bang and change the set at intermission?"

"Jory, that is so, so not how this works."

"Right. I know that. Hmm."

"I wish Hunter were here. He'd figure this out in a second."

"Yeah, me too," Jory said.

"It seems like his trials are as much a trial for us, learning to pick up his slack."

"It'll be back to normal soon," Jory said, really hoping it would be.

"I'll take a look at what we have so far on the candelabra. Maybe inspiration will strike," said Aziz as he emerged from the wing and tried to stay out of the way of the actors while checking out the half-completed candelabra set piece.

Meanwhile, Kevin and Chloe were getting to the good part.

PHANTASM:
MY DEBUT COMPOSITION
CANNOT FACE DERISION
AND THUS I NEED A STAR
WITH A VOICE LIKE CAVIAR
AND THAT IS YOU, MY CRYSTALLINE
SING TRUE, MY CRYSTALLINE!

CRYSTALLINE:
YOU ARE A GHOST, BUT AS MY HOST
YOU HAVE BEEN KIND, AND SO I FIND
MYSELF INCLINED TO SING YOUR SONG
AS STRONGLY AS I CAN!
YOU LED ME HERE, AND IN MY FEAR
I NEARLY FLED, BUT IN MY HEAD
I HEARD A TUNE AND IN THE MOONLIGHT
I SHALL SING AGAIN!

BRING ME THE SCORE!

I WILL SING UNTIL MOR-NING!

But when Kevin, as the Phantasm, reached into the desk set piece for the score prop, it was not there. He fished around in the drawer a bit as Chloe looked on expectantly, still trying to keep the scene going, but it was nowhere to be found. The accompanist vamped the same four bars of music again and again. The Phantasm lost his ghostly mystique and seemed much more like a teenage boy embarrassed in front of a roomful of people.

"HOLD!" Kevin shouted, tearing the signature Phantasm mask off in a rage. "Can I get a stage manager, please?!"

Aziz shot Jory a look in the wing. Jory shook his head emphatically. Aziz took a deep breath and stepped onto the stage.

"The stage managers are busy right now working on . . . an effect," he lied. "Is there something I can help you with?"

Kevin's eyes narrowed.

"Well, what about Hunter? He is usually next in command, right?"

"He's also . . . busy right now."

"Does ANYONE WORK HERE?!"

". . . Me. As I said. So, can I help you with something?"

"Well, we've got a CRUCIAL prop missing. I was told ALL props would be in place today! It's only the very piece of MUSIC that the entire SHOW is ABOUT!"

"Well . . ." Aziz quickly scanned the wings, looking for Sasha. Props were his department, and the missing score was definitely his mistake. Aziz spotted him downstage right, building something. He squinted and could see it was a doll-sized house but with spooky-looking, tiny sheets draped over tiny furniture and cotton cobwebs everywhere. Sasha was putting the finishing touch on it—a big sign hanging above it that read HAUNT ME in large red letters. Aziz dropped his head.

"It was my bad," he lied. "I was thinking about the candelabra effect and got distracted, I guess. It won't happen again."

"Thank you," Kevin said through teeth clenched into a not very convincing smile. "This is the biggest show we've ever attempted, and we need everyone working at their best."

"Of course, Kevin. I'm so sorry." Aziz was humiliated, but he would survive—and he was glad to take the blow for his friend.

"We're due for a ten-minute break anyway," Kevin said. "That's TEN, people! Not ELEVEN, but TEN!"

"Thank you, Ten!" some actors called back.

Kevin swept away to regain his composure and become the Phantasm again. Aziz sighed, crisis averted.

"Okay, I'm calling bull." Chloe had been watching the whole exchange. "You're working on a set effect *and* are in charge of props? Seems like a lot for one Backstager."

"We have a lot of ground to cover on this one," Aziz said.

"Or maybe you have someone to protect?" Chloe said, a twinkle in her eye.

"I don't know what you—"

"No, I think it's cool, you taking the fall for one of your own. That could have gotten really ugly, but you handled it so well. You're a real leader . . . Sorry, I don't know if we've actually spoken yet. What's your name?"

"Aziz."

"Nice to meet you, Aziz, I'm Chloe. Sorry we didn't talk sooner. It's so hard for the actors to get any personal time with the Backstagers."

"Well, I don't think many of the actors make much of an effort."

"You might be right about that. But have you tried saying hi yourself? It works both ways, you know."

"Ha, me and actors don't really mix." Aziz gestured to a corner of the auditorium where the ensemble boys were doing some strange ritual that would terrify a sensible person but in the theater counted as a warm-up.

Chloe laughed. "We can be a little silly, but that's part of our charm, I think. Don't you wish you could just look stupid like that and not care?"

"I looked pretty stupid just now. I'm sure all of the actors are talking about how annoyed they are that there was a technical glitch that got in the way of *their* show."

"Sounds like you are being awfully judgmental about the people you *think* are judging you. Maybe you should get out of your bubble a bit. Maybe you'd see we're not all so bad."

That hit Aziz in a way he didn't expect. He thought instantly back to a time a few months ago when his parents had pulled him out of drama club after the Backstagers disappeared and made him try track, where his two younger brothers could keep an eye on him. He was no athlete and the whole thing was an exhausting fiasco, but he did think at the time that it was kind of nice to hang with a group of guys who didn't regularly fight literal ghosts or debate the best brand of spike tape to use. He had felt like a normal teenager, if only for a couple of weeks.

"I'm gonna hit the water fountain before time's up," Chloe said. "Oh, and that candelabra effect? Put the whole set piece on a rolling pallet with a one-inch lip all the way around. Control the explosion so the pieces all fall on the pallet, and then just wheel the whole thing off in the transition." She started off.

"I thought this was your first time in a show," Aziz said, gobsmacked.

"It is," Chloe said. "Just an idea."

She walked off into the wings as Aziz looked back to the candelabra set.

Once safely in the wings, Chloe slowed her breath and honed her focus. She was on a hunt, but it wasn't the water fountain she was hunting for. She moved purposefully toward the back wall of the stage, her eyes darting about wildly in the darkness. Then she spotted it—the stage door. She raced up to it, but her heart sank when she saw the thick padlock holding it closed. She pulled a pin out of her silver hair and instantly set to work at picking the lock, a steely determination in her eyes. A boyish voice from behind interrupted her work.

"Are you looking for the ghost, too?"

She spun around, startled. It was Sasha, beaming up at her.

"It isn't back there, it's out here somewhere, but I built a house for it to haunt and left it some malted milk balls—do you think ghosts like malted milk balls?"

He gazed at her, anxiously awaiting her thoughts on a ghost's favorite confection.

"What? Um, sure." She hid the hairpin behind her back and tried to focus all of her body language to get Sasha to leave. Unsurprisingly, he did not catch on.

"Or do you maybe think they like something see-through? Like gummy bears? Or is that weird for them, like cannibalism or something?"

"I DON'T KNOW!" Chloe barked. Sasha's eyes grew somehow wider, and she knew she had lost her temper.

"That is," she recovered, "your guess is as good as mine. Maybe go find all the kinds of candy you can and do an experiment?"

"That's a GREAT idea! I shall conduct an EXPERIMENT and I shall report my findings as soon as I can!"

". . . Awesome. So . . ."

"I am going to help FIX a mess, not just cause one!"

"Great . . ."

Sasha smiled at her for a few awkward moments of total silence before darting off with the speed of a cartoon chase in search of candy for the ghost.

Chloe sighed and resumed her work, now growing frantic. She felt something click within the lock and pulled down hard, but it did not come free. She let out an exasperated grunt. She was so close.

"That's ten!" Kevin shouted from onstage. Chloe's shoulders fell. Too late. She dashed back through the wings, putting on her phony ingénue smile like a mask before emerging into the light.

"Do we have the correct prop this time?" Kevin asked, trying to maintain his composure but barely masking his annoyance.

"All set," Aziz said, producing the prop score and slapping it down on the organ set piece with more than a little extra force. He shot Chloe a look, an almost imperceptible eye roll, and she smiled. Her smile changed into something more serious, though, when Aziz turned to go back to his work on the candelabra, revealing the ring of keys hanging from his back belt loop.

CHAPTER 9

THE AIR WAS ALIVE WITH THE UNMISTAKABLE HUM OF THE OPENING NIGHT of a musical.

The sound of audience members quietly buzzing with anticipation is something like music to most theater people, but to Hunter, it was the sound of a ticking clock. That countdown was ticking away in imaginary red numbers, falling one by one through the back of his mind as he tried to remain present and attentive for fight call—the last-minute rehearsal where the actors went through the motions of their stage fights for safety.

There were a thousand and one things to think about, but Hunter tried to push all of them out of his mind, at least momentarily, as he focused on the slow-motion punches and kicks of two actors working on a choreographed brawl on the bare stage.

"Good," he said, attempting to maintain a tone of enthusiasm despite his exhaustion. "Just make sure those slaps are on a nice wide angle at an arm's length away. Don't get caught up in the moment—the audience's eyes don't work as fast as you think. They want to believe it. Eye contact. Safety."

Two faceless actors nodded and faded away into nothingness.

Hunter looked down at his notepad. Prop check—check. Sound check—check. Fog and haze—check. Pyro—check. Fight call—finally, check.

Was that everything? His mind was mush. He tried to go over the list again, but he kept losing his place, like when you've just woken up from a wonderful dream and you are trying to remember the details as they drift further and further away. He decided he must've done everything. Looking down at his watch, he saw that he was out of time anyway—7:29 p.m. on the dot. He raced back into the wings to his calling desk and picked up a radio handset. He took a deep breath and depressed the call button.

"Good evening, gentlemen . . . and lady, this is your half-hour call. One half hour until the top of the show. Half hour."

He released the button and slumped back into his chair, completely depleted.

"STOP." The disappointed voice rippled through the theater as everything around Hunter—the calling desk, the curtains, the stage floor, the sound of the audience—all dissolved into the formless whiteness of the Training Room, a blank space that the stage managers could mold into any challenge they could imagine.

Crap, Hunter thought, too tired to be as devastated as he might have been a few hours ago.

"Almost, Hunt, but you forgot a tiny little something." Timothy appeared in a whoosh, his tall blondness cutting a colorful column through the endless white. "The sign-in sheet? You know, that little thing that tells you whether or not all of your actors have actually shown up to work that night? If you'd have checked it, you would have noticed that Kevin McQueen is not signed in. I'm curious, how were you planning to put on a production of *Phantasm* without a PHANTASM?!"

"Come on, Tim, he's wiped, look at the guy." Jamie's beard appeared first, followed by his concerned expression. "You're being hard on him."

"Because I know he's better than this," Timothy said, looking at Hunter with an equal, if different, concern. "Come on, Hunter, the sign-in sheet is basic stuff. Is something going on?"

"No," Hunter said quickly, more a reflex than a real answer. "I just got confused. It won't happen again. Let's start over. From the top. I'm ready this time."

"You need rest," Jamie said sternly. He said it to Hunter, though he was looking right at Timothy. Hunter felt like crying but kept it together. Timothy took a breath.

"I'm sorry, Hunter. I know we've been pushing you. But St. Genesius needs a great stage manager after we leave, and I know you have the potential to be truly great," Timothy said.

"Take the night," Jamie said. "Deal with whatever is on your mind and come in fresh tomorrow. And please, get some good sleep."

Jamie reached his hand out and knocked on a spot in the endless white. The spot became a door. He opened it, revealing the starry darkness beyond—the tunnels of the backstage.

The three boys walked back through the tunnels toward the Club Room in silence as Hunter's exhaustion gave way to embarrassment. He knew exactly what was on his mind, distracting him from his training—Jory.

He had missed Jory so much over the last few weeks. Every time the stage manager training became too much for him, he wanted to call Jory and vent for hours, but there was always something else to study. Being a stage manager literally meant knowing everything about the-ater—you had to know what to do if any single depart-ment had an emergency, from lighting to wardrobe to the printing of the programs. You had to deal with the actors when they were sick or nervous or having a fight with some other actor. You had to control each and every technical cue in the show, which meant taking respon-sibility for the work of every single person involved in the production. If the lighting designer's hard work got messed up, it was your fault. If a wedding cake that the prop master spent hours building out of foam didn't get preset properly and thus wasn't seen on stage, it was your fault. If an actor got sick and the understudy didn't know where to stand to be in his light for his climactic moment, it was your fault.

All of this weighed on Hunter, but rather than whine about it to his boyfriend, he chose to keep working, to get on top of it and be the best. He realized, though, that in trying to not burden Jory with his complaining, he had actually cut off contact from Jory all but completely. He vowed to be better about this from now on, starting with the date he and Jory were supposed to have in a few hours.

"What time is it?" Hunter asked blearily as they finally crossed the Unsafe line into the Club Room and back to the mundane world of the St. Genesius auditorium.

"Nine forty-five," Jamie replied through a yawn. "Like I said, you need to rest."

Hunter's blood turned to ice water. He was supposed to meet Jory at the ice cream shop at 8:30. The backstage had once again messed with his internal clock and what had felt like forty minutes had actually been five hours.

"I gotta run," Hunter explained as he clumsily tugged on his coat and scurried up the stairs toward the auditorium level.

"REST," Jamie called after him, sounding eerily like his own mother.

Hunter ran all the way from St. Genesius to the downtown strip mall ice cream shop where Jory was waiting. He was completely drained from hours and hours of training, but his fear of disappointing Jory was a new fire in his furnace, and he raced at an uncharacteristic clip.

When he finally reached the shop, sweating like a marathon runner crossing the finish line, he was greeted not by cheering onlookers and flashing cameras, but by the saddest thing he had ever seen. There, sitting alone in a window seat, illuminated by a flickering halogen light, was Jory, filling his spoon with melted ice cream and pouring it back into its soggy cup, again and again.

Hunter tamed his shock of hair into its normal sculpture and entered the shop with a ring of the doorbell. Jory looked up at him and smiled weakly.

"Hey!" Hunter said, trying not to sound like a crazy person or the biggest jerk in the world while simultaneously sweating his guts out and wondering if he might need medical attention from the physical strain he had just endured. "Sorry I'm so late. I was—"

"Training," Jory interrupted. "I know. How did it go?"

"It was fine, but forget that, let's talk about anything else. What are we having?!"

"It was mint chocolate chip, but it's more of a soup now."

"It's okay! I like it that way!"

"Seriously, Hunter?"

"No, I mean it! It's getting kinda cold out for ice cream anyway."

"Yeah, I guess ice cream was a stupid idea."

"That's not what I meant, Jory . . ."

Jory looked down at the mint chocolate puddle and fought back tears.

"Jory, what's wrong?"

"Well . . ." Jory gathered his strength and tried to find the words to say what he meant and not what he didn't. "I know how important the training is. I would never want to get in the way of that. Still, it's been kind of lonely without you around so much. I feel so stupid even saying that—I don't want you to think that I'm the kind of guy who can't have a life if his boyfriend isn't around every second of the day, but I'm still new here and I don't really have many friends."

"What? Jory, the Backstagers adore you! They love hanging out with you!"

"Well, yeah, but it can be hard," Jory said. He tried for a moment to meet Hunter's concerned gaze but knew that it would put him over the edge. He kept his eyes safely fixed on the counter in front of him as he continued. "Aziz and Sasha have been friends forever and play the same games and stuff. We all know Beckett prefers to be on his own in the booth. And Timothy and Jamie have college prep *in addition* to training you. I just kinda fall through the cracks."

"Oh my gosh, Jory, I'm so sorry you've been feeling like that—I had no idea. Do you want me to tell the guys I need to lighten up on training hours?"

"Of course not! I would never want to hold you back, Hunter. This is your dream. I would feel terrible if you weren't focused on it one hundred percent."

Hunter thought about his flub at training today. He knew Jory was right, and he knew that he definitely wasn't operating at one hundred percent right now.

"Actually," Hunter said, finding the words slowly, "my focus has been a problem. Today I made a really stupid mistake during a practice run. Jamie could tell something was bothering me and I said I was fine, but when he said it, I knew it was this. Missing you."

"Hunter, that breaks my heart. I don't want to be something that is causing you even more stress."

"No, it's not like that at all. I just feel so awful that I don't have more time for us."

"No, I feel awful that I'm something you need to make time for."

"Well that's . . . tricky."

". . . Yeah."

The boys sat at the counter for a long moment, stuck. The halogen bulb above hummed and clicked as it flickered, but everything else was horribly quiet.

"Hey, guys," the shopkeeper called from his counter, "I gotta close up, I'm sorry. I stayed open as late as I could."

"No problem, thanks," Jory said, grateful to have something break the silence.

They threw the melted ice cream away and walked out into the crisp winter night. The sky above was something like the starry sky that blanketed the tunnels of the backstage, but this sky felt less magically vast and more darkly empty. The shopkeeper flicked off the light, locked up the store, and headed to his car, giving Hunter and Jory a sympathetic nod on his way. Now it was deadly quiet. Jory spoke at last.

"Hunter, I won't be able to sleep if I think I'm getting in the way of you doing your very best at the trials. It's too important, and I care too much about you to be in the way. You have to focus on it completely. And maybe it is a good thing that I will have to find myself at Genesius independent from you. I'm brand-new here. Maybe a little time apart from each other will be good for both of us."

"You mean like a break?" Hunter asked. That last word hung horribly in the air.

"I guess I do, yeah. Until you're done with the trials. I won't be a boyfriend you have to make time for, I'll be just another one of the Backstagers. Just for now."

"Okay. You're probably right. Okay." Hunter was trying to sound fine, but even though he knew this was the right thing, it wasn't at all what he wanted. All he wanted was to go back in time and share that ice cream like they'd planned and talk about normal kid stuff.

"Okay. Well, get some rest and I'll see you around," Jory said. He extended his hand for a handshake, trying to lighten the moment with a joke. He smiled. Hunter took his hand and pulled him into a bear hug. They held on to each other tightly as the cold wind caught in the trees around the empty parking lot. Eventually, they let go and went their separate ways.

Jory made it about two hundred yards before he felt warm tears well up in the cold air. They weren't breakup tears—it wasn't exactly a breakup and he knew he was doing the right thing. They were something deeper. It was the relief of saying out loud what he had been pushing down for weeks now—he was still adjusting to this new place, and it was hard, and it was going to take time. It turned out that confiding in Hunter was what he needed most.

As sad as he was to put a hold on things, he felt something shift inside him. It was growing up.

He felt a buzz in his pocket. Oh gosh, he thought, please don't be Hunter saying he regretted their decision. He took his phone out. It was worse.

MISSED CALLS: 10
TEXTS:
Mom: Jory it's 11:30 where ARE YOU CALL ME RIGHTTHISINSTANT

"Hey, Mom." Jory had called her before he even finished reading the message. "Sorry, I got caught up with some school stuff . . . No, not Backstager stuff . . . health class stuff. A paper on . . . B.O.? Anyway, I'm almost home, sorry to worry you, BYE!" He hung up before she could quiz him any more and took off in a sprint toward home.

He took the shortcut through the woods—it was a bit creepy at night, but honestly, after getting lost in the backstage, it really didn't seem so bad. Plus, absolutely nothing was scarier than his mom when she was angry.

His lungs stung in the winter wind, but he was nearly there—he just needed to pass the clearing and then it was a straight shot to his backyard. He rounded a few trees and leaped over logs, stones, and streams, never slowing his pace until he was met in the clearing by a sight that froze him dead in his tracks.

In the center of the clearing, beneath that black sky, sat an even darker figure, hooded, surrounded by a circle of half-melted white candles. Before it lay a strange collection of mysterious-looking materials. There was an altar of some kind with a bowl of a pungent herbal mixture burning on it, its smoke curling into the air in ghostly tendrils. The figure looked up from the altar, straight at Jory. It stood. Jory screamed his lungs out and took off in the other direction. The figure gave chase.

"Help me! Someone! It's a ghost!" Jory cried. He bounded back into the woods, searching for cover, but the figure was right on his heels, running after him with arms outstretched. Jory tripped on a snarl of branches, crashing to the forest floor.

"No, please!" Jory pleaded, raising his arms to cover his head, awaiting certain doom.

"Jory!" the figure shouted as it caught up to him. "It's me! Gosh, are you okay? That looked like it hurt, dude!"

Pulling his hood down, the ghostly figure haunting the woods revealed himself to be Reo, the witch. He reached out his hand to Jory, who took it, still stunned and winded. Reo pulled him up off the ground and dusted leaves from his hair and clothes.

"I am SO sorry! I really didn't think anyone ever came out this way. Especially not this time of night," Reo said.

"N-no, I'm sorry," Jory stammered, ". . . to interrupt. You just looked—"

"Terrifying? Yeah, I know it all looks a little spooky."

"What . . . what were you doing?"

"Moonbathing!"

"What?"

"Or, that's what I call it. It's a full moon tonight—see?"

Jory looked up and noticed for the first time that the moon was like a perfect spotlight in the sky, pouring silver light into the clearing.

"The moon is very important to witches," Reo explained. "We try to live in rhythm with her phases—new moons are for beginnings, waxing moons are for growth, waning moons are for cleaning, dark moons are for rest, and when she's full?" Reo looked up at the sky affectionately. "She's at her peak power. Full moons are for wishing. I like to come out here and try to soak up some of that power, so I can carry it with me to school for when the bullies come around, or there's a pop quiz or I get picked last in gym or whatever. I can think back on nights like this and feel her power backing me up. Moonbathing."

Jory looked toward Reo's setup in the clearing. On second viewing, it was less spooky and actually quite beautiful, the candlelight casting a warm, pulsing circle on the forest floor.

"And what's all this stuff?" Jory asked, walking with crunching steps back into the clearing, toward the inviting amber light.

"The candles and incense? For protection. I know this town is, like, the safest, most boring place on Earth, but the woods kind of freak me out at night."

Jory had to chuckle at the idea of a witch afraid of the woods and the dark.

"Anyway," Reo said. "I know it's pretty weird. I'm sorry I scared you."

"It's lovely," Jory said. "I could definitely use some moon power sometimes. Tonight, for sure."

"Why don't you join me, then?" Reo said, his eyes lighting up.

"Are you sure? I wouldn't want to, like, take any of your moonbeams."

"I think there are enough for both of us. She's really got her shine on tonight."

"My mom is waiting for me at home."

"Just for five minutes. You can get some good moonbeams in five minutes."

"What do I do?"

"Step into the circle here and get comfortable."

They stepped into the center of the circle of candles and sat, cross-legged, back to back. The incense swirled around them, fragrant and inviting.

"Now," Reo said, "shut your eyes. Feel her up there, lighting up the night for everyone. And when you're ready, introduce yourself."

". . . Hi, Moon, I'm Jor—"

"Not like that," Reo chuckled. "Just think it. She'll understand."

"Sorry. Right."

"And then, once you do . . . just listen."

The boys sat in silence on the forest floor, listening to the mysterious chatter of the forest around them.

If you're up there listening, Jory thought, *I could use some help right now.* But then, sensing Reo just behind him, having his own private conversation with the night, a new friend who had literally appeared in the darkness, he knew help had arrived before he even had to ask.

CHAPTER 10

HOLY CRAP, CHLOE HAD BEEN RIGHT.

The candelabra set piece exploded gorgeously, and all of the pieces fell neatly into the pallet that Aziz had constructed at her suggestion, making for an easy transition into the next scene.

Rehearsal was about to begin and actors milled about the stage, performing strange facial stretches, doing vocal sirens, and drinking what seemed like excessive, possibly dangerous, amounts of water.

Aziz, working alone in an upstage corner, had a private moment of celebration as his final test of the effect went perfectly. Or what he thought was a private moment. A voice behind him cut his celebration short.

"Aziz, that looks fantastic!" It was Chloe, her silver hair framing the glow of her smile.

"Thanks. Your idea was a great one."

"Oh, you would have figured it out; you were almost there. But I'm glad I could help."

"I don't know, man, a pallet with a lip on it? That's really good thinking. You ever think about Backstaging?"

"I have my place onstage."

"Maybe you should get out of your *bubble* sometime," he joked.

"Touché. What about you, would you ever try Onstaging?"

"Me?! Oh gosh, no. That would be a disaster."

"Why? You love theater."

"I love *working on* theater."

"That is loving theater, weirdo. You love theater, and you demonstrated the other day how much of a leader you are, taking responsibility for that prop mess-up."

"That was nothing."

"That was amazing, Aziz! You should take more credit for all the work you do around here. I get that being a Backstager is about being invisible, but I don't know, for me, I think it's nice to get some credit for my hard work every now and then. I don't think there is anything wrong with that. Otherwise, your work just *happens* under the cover of darkness and no one ever stops to think about who made it happen. You're like a ghost."

Aziz's ears pricked up. Before he could think too hard about what she had said, Blake McQueen swept onto the stage, eclipsing all the energy in the room with his dramatic entrance.

"ACTORS!" he bellowed. "Today we are tackling the climactic sewer scene, in which the dashing Rupert, played by yours truly, duels thrillingly with the Phantasm as the townsfolk descend into his lair, torches blazing. We will need everyone's best work for such a complex scene—a real sense of *risk* and *play*! Thus, for today's warm-up, I propose we . . . PASS THE IMPULSE!"

The room squealed with excitement as the actors formed a circle. Chloe's eyes flashed as she looked at Aziz the way a cat looks at a mouse just before it pounces.

"Yes," she said. "This is perfect. You're trying it."

"WHAT?!" Aziz would under no circumstances be trying it.

"Warm up with us. You'll love it."

"I don't know what I'm doing."

"There's nothing to know! Come on."

"Chloe, I can't."

"That attitude is your worst enemy, Aziz. You can do anything. Get over here!"

She pulled him into the circle of actors the way a mom pulls a stubborn kid into a dentist's office.

The actors (plus Aziz) held hands and took a few deep breaths all together. Aziz felt ridiculous and a bit like he was joining a cult, but he looked pitifully to Chloe and she gave him an encouraging nod.

After they broke hands, one of the actors made a terrifying, abstract wail, flinging his body into an unnatural contortion. Aziz wondered for a moment if he had been possessed by the ghost. But then the actor next to him made the same bizarre sound and movement and then the next actor did the same.

As this animalistic gesture made its way around the circle, Chloe leaned over and explained that each actor made up an impulse—literally the first sound and movement that came to mind—and every other actor had to mimic it, passing it around, until it made it back to whoever started it. Then the next actor would come up with a new impulse and pass that one around. It taught them to take risks and let their creativity out, unfiltered.

The impulse came around to Chloe and she mimicked the flailing perfectly without any self-consciousness. Then it was Aziz's turn. He gave a sort of fifty-percent version, fearing he would look stupid if he did it full out. But the funny thing was, with everyone committing to the exercise with such abandon, doing it timidly was what actually made him stand out and look stupid. Looking stupid was the point.

When the next impulse came around, a sort of tongue-wagging maniac dance, he tried harder to nail the details and not worry so much about what people would think of it. By his third or fourth turn, he was truly enjoying it and feeling freer than he had in ages. That is, until the time came for him to come up with an impulse of his own.

When it was his turn to actually launch a movement, he froze up and the game came to a conspicuous halt. He turned to Chloe, suddenly terrified. She gave him a look that said, "You're on your own, dude!"

He managed to muster a tiny ". . . hey . . ." with an accompanying humiliated wave of his hand and slump of his shoulders. As he saw his timid ". . . hey . . ." mirrored by actor after actor with each one completely nailing his expression of wanting to disappear into the floor, he had to laugh in spite of himself. Everyone joined him in laughter.

When the game circled back around to Aziz, he mirrored the "hey" as they did, overdoing his shyness, making fun of himself perfectly. Everyone cheered. Chloe slapped him on the back affectionately.

Maybe there is something to this Onstager thing, he thought.

"Okay, everyone," Kevin McQueen said firmly, not wanting Aziz to hold the spotlight for too long, "let's get started. Can we have some shadowy light for the sewer scene, please?"

He waited a moment for the lights to shift from the white work light to something more atmospheric, but it didn't. Everyone looked up to the light booth.

"I SAID, can we have some sewer light, please?"

Again no shift. Aziz raised an eyebrow.

"Ugh, what is HAPPENING around here?" Blake threw his hands up in frustration.

"I'll get it," Aziz said, throwing a look to Chloe.

She smiled as he passed on his way to the booth. She watched the keys hanging off his back pocket flash in the work light.

Aziz was still buzzing from his first foray into theater games, but that joy in his mind was clouded as he wondered what they were all wondering: Where the heck was Beckett?

CHAPTER 11

BAILEY TOOK ONE FINAL LOOK AT HER FRAMED *LEASE* POSTER, its margins full of messages and signatures.

You were sooooooo amazing! Can't wait
until the next show! —xoxo Bradley

Girl, that vocal you were serving!
See you on Broadway —Rex

I have notes but overall, well done, Bailey.
Yours, Blake McQueen

She chucked it into a big cardboard box, along with all of her other theater memorabilia. The walls of her second-story bedroom looked bare without the show posters, cast photos, and paper-plate awards, but they also felt clean and clear.

The artifacts from her tenure as leading lady of the St. Genesius Drama Club now filled her with embarrassment and regret rather than nostalgia and happiness. She was ashamed that the mere presence of this stuff upset her so much. She had tried to get past it, but every night when she came straight home after school instead of staying extra hours working to mount her dream show at St. Genesius, the photos mocked her and sent her spiraling into an endless recap of the day she had blown the audition. She had taken for granted that she would get the lead once again and had already envisioned what her performance would be like and how it would feel to sing those legendary songs in front of an audience. Now the show that used to be her favorite haunted her every night. She needed a fresh start.

Would she try basketball? She was tallish and not totally terrible at sports. But if this was how she handled not getting one role, how would she feel when her team suffered the inevitable losses that all teams endure? Maybe student government . . . No, elections seemed like auditions but a billion times worse. Choir? Definitely not.

She found some peace as she plunked the framed photos and posters into the box, the steady rhythm taking the things that pained her further and further away. When she paused her work momentarily, she was jolted back into consciousness because the plunking rhythm continued without her. After a moment, she realized the plunks were not coming from the cardboard box, but from her bedroom window.

She tiptoed over to the window to investigate the source of the sound. She had almost reached it when outside, a pebble flew up from the ground below and smacked against the glass: *plunk*. She staggered back.

"Ugh, stupid kids!" Now she was angry. The last thing she needed right now were neighborhood tweens being obnoxious. She raced to the window and opened it in a fury, ready to serve some swift justice to the troublemakers. Only instead of troublemakers below her window, she found Beckett.

It wasn't everyday Beckett. This was fancy, I've-watched-too-many-'80s-movies Beckett. Under his winter parka, she could see that he was wearing a button-down shirt and a little bow tie. Clean, unwrinkled ones, at that. Bailey had to laugh, he looked so unlike himself. He looked decaffeinated.

He motioned to her to come down. She nodded and shut the window and lowered the blinds. Once clear of the sight of her, Beckett stopped holding his breath and allowed himself a few of the frenzied, terrified gasps he had been stifling. He blotted his brow with a tissue from his pocket.

It was close to freezing outside, but he was sweating bullets. He composed himself again quickly as Bailey crept through the front door in a robe and slippers.

"Beckett!" she whispered, pulling him in for a tight hug. "What are you doing here?! Don't you have rehearsal?"

"Oh . . . yeah. Yeah, I actually ducked out for a minute."

"That's not like you."

"I know. A lot of things lately aren't like me. I came up with a whole new cabling system for the light and sound wires, but it didn't bring me any joy. I was up to eight Diet Cokes a day and then I quit cold turkey. Blake McQueen was walking around for a whole rehearsal with a booger in his nose and I couldn't even laugh. I can't study, I can't sleep. I just keep thinking about that day—that day that I ruined your audition."

"Oh, Beckett," Bailey said. A gust of winter wind swept across her front yard, catching her long, sleek hair. She pulled her robe tight around her, but the sight of Beckett warmed her considerably. "You didn't ruin it."

"Yes, I did. We both know it."

"I didn't have the high note. That had nothing to do with you or that stupid light falling. Which, honestly, is worse. If it was because of your mistake, I would forgive you. I know you wouldn't do that on purpose. But it was because of me and my ability. I just wasn't good enough, and that wouldn't have been any different even if the light hadn't fallen."

"Well . . ." Beckett tugged on one of his plugs nervously, carefully crafting his next words. "I think that's good news, actually."

"What?"

"It's not that you're not good enough. You've gotten so many lead roles, you can't brush that off as a fluke. But this role is for a soprano and maybe you just aren't a soprano. I'm sure that can be hard, but I don't think a soprano would have sounded very good on the *Lease* score. Those songs are for belters. And I think I'd rather hear a true belter nail the *Lease* score and crack on the *Phantasm* score than hear someone who could kind of get away with both not be really great at either. Your voice might not be perfect for every show, but for certain shows—definitely for everything I've seen you in—it's absolutely magic."

Bailey smiled for what felt like the first time in weeks.

"That's really, really beautiful, Beckett. Thank you. To be clear, I never, ever blamed you. Sleep! Study! But maybe don't get back on the Diet Coke. At least, not as much."

He chuckled. "I'll try."

"I have really missed you, though. The drama club shows were our chance to hang. We gotta get better about that."

"I'd like that. Definitely." He died a little inside but tried to contain himself and play it cool.

"Out of curiosity, who ended up getting the part? I thought I was the last girl trying out."

"Some girl named Chloe Murphy. She's great, actually. Not that you want to hear that."

Bailey's smile faded slightly. "Chloe Murphy? With the silver hair?"

"Yeah."

"But . . . Chloe Murphy isn't an Onstager. She's a Backstager."

"You must be confused."

"No, I'm sure of it. She replaced you, actually, when you transferred. I remember that her hair reflected in the light too much and the Penitent stage managers made her wear a hat."

"Well, maybe she wanted to try something new."

"But that's not all," Bailey said, her expression growing increasingly confused. "She only lasted one show with the stage crew before she dropped out to be homeschooled—less than a semester. There was a death in her family—her little sister, I think. She's no longer a student at Penitent Angels."

Beckett was at a loss. The cold wind howled across Bailey's lawn, like a ghost wailing in the night.

"But if she's not an Onstager and not even a current student," Beckett pondered aloud, "what is she doing acting in the Genesius musical?"

CHAPTER 12

November 3

I can't believe I'm actually picking this thing up again. The words seem like the writing of a total stranger. Was I really this happy and carefree? Did I actually care about the production of a musical? Did I truly get upset with Phoebe for things like going into my room and borrowing my hairbrush?

The author of that diary died with Phoebe. This will no longer be a diary about frivolous teenage things like crushes and homework, but a research notebook as I set out to find my sister. I can feel her still. I know she is out there.

Up until recently, research on ghosts and paranormal activity led me to ridiculous fictions about lamps falling off of tables and footsteps in attics. Nothing about how to get in contact, or where. Recently, however, something (Phoebe herself, leading me?) caused me to cross-reference ghosts and theater. Theater was one of the only things Phoebe and I had in common, even though she preferred the onstage and I preferred the backstage. I thought maybe I could find her there.

One book, In the Ghostlight, was particularly illuminating. It speculates that ghosts manifest in theaters easily because theaters are spaces between worlds—the place where the imaginations of the playwright, the designers, the actors, and the audience all mash together and become real. That is why theaters require a ghost light left on all night, to keep spirits from crossing over and moving in.

I knew immediately that a theater would be the ideal place to make contact with her. My challenge now is finding some way to get access to a theater, alone, in the middle of the night, so I can turn off the ghost light and make contact. If Mom hadn't pulled me from Penitent, this would be easy—I had my own set of keys to the auditorium! Now I'm going to have to get creative . . .

December 15
Checklist
1. A disguise. Be invisible.
2. The Spirit Board for making contact once alone
3. A snack, in case I get hungry

It seems extraordinarily lucky that St. Genesius happens to be having a cast party so close to the beginning of my research. The auditorium will be wide-open and everyone will be distracted. All I have to do is sneak in unnoticed, wait until everyone leaves, turn off the ghost light, and make contact with the Spirit Board I bought. That last bit has me a bit worried—I always thought of those things as fake party tricks for kids, but after all of my research, I haven't found a better plan. I am anxious to report my findings.

December 16
MAJOR BREAKTHROUGHS. CONFIDENTIAL INFORMA-TION BELOW!

Last night was an unbelievable success. It was almost derailed when some of the Genesius actors found where I had stashed the Spirit Board and started playing with it, but I managed to scare them off of it. Just as they were starting to freak themselves out with questions, I got the idea to sneak out of my hiding spot and smash the ghost light with a hammer. They got totally spooked and I had taken care of the ghost light—two birds with one stone!

After everyone left, I retrieved the board and input my greeting—"P-H-O-E-B-E. A-R-E Y-O-U T-H-E-R-E?" I was shocked when after just a few moments, the planchette slid beneath my hands to "YES." I used the board to ask where she was and she answered, "C-L-O-S-E."

I can't tell you what that felt like, to have been right. To have actually made contact, after all this time. But suddenly I grew wary—maybe my hands were just subconsciously spelling out the answers I wanted—needed—to hear. To test this, I asked her if there was any way I could see her and took my hands off of the planchette.

It started to move on its own.

"YES."

I asked how, and letter by letter, Phoebe told me that in the auditorium, when the ghost light was off, she could speak to me through the board, but in the backstage, she could manifest completely. She gave me a mission: Get into the backstage, go as deep as I can possibly go, and find a theater. In that theater, there will be another, larger ghost light. If I shatter that ghost light as I did the one that was onstage, then she would be free to manifest in the backstage and we could travel back to the real world together. We said goodbye and I collected the board and planchette and made my escape.

Obviously, I have too many thoughts swirling in my head to accurately put down here and I certainly won't be sleeping tonight, but it is clear that I must have more regular access to the St. Genesius stage and I must find my way into their backstage as soon as possible. This was the last cast party for a while, so I'm going to have to come up with something else.

Phoebe, sit tight! Your big sister is coming to rescue you!

January 3

I swear, Phoebe must be working from beyond to help me, because Genesius just announced they are doing *Phantasm* for the winter musical. This is significant, because as much as I despise that corny show, Mom made me sing those songs in voice lessons every week until I finally told her I was giving up singing to be a Backstager. I know I can nail those songs.

Crystalline is the one role I could have possibly won over the other girls and THIS winter, they choose to do *Phantasm*? That's got to be some kind of influence from beyond.

My plan is to wait until all of the other girls have auditioned and left before making my entrance. The female lead must be a current student at Penitent Angels, so if I'm discovered by the other Penitent girls, the plan is ruined. I saw the sign-up sheet online—I know none of the others can handle the high note.

My only concern is Bailey Brentwood. She has gotten the female lead of every Genesius show she's auditioned for. I have always really liked and respected her, but seeing Phoebe again is the most important thing right now. As much as I hate to get in Bailey's way, I can't let anything stop me from rescuing my sister . . .

January 8

The audition is today and I am reminded why I was never an Onstager. This frilly dress, this cheesy song, this fake smile I have to put on to be what they want me to be—I hope I don't barf in the middle of the audition.

Still, I know I can endure it for Phoebe's sake. She loved performing, so I can, too. It just goes to show that maybe everything does happen for a reason. All those years of voice lessons that I absolutely hated . . . who knew they would turn out to be so useful?

However, I still can't understand what the reason was for Phoebe to be taken from me so young. That had to be a mistake of the universe. One I intend to correct today.

><

January 8, later

You know the feeling of winning and losing at the same time?

Long story short, I got the role. At what cost, though?

Poor Bailey Brentwood. When I crawled up into the light grid, I almost didn't go through with it. Even as I was loosening the clamp that held the light in place, my mind was saying, "STOP. What are you doing? This isn't you, Chloe." But then I thought about Phoebe and I just . . . acted. It was like I was outside of my body, watching myself.

I made certain the light fell a safe distance away from her—she was never in any real danger. Still, she was completely humiliated when she couldn't recover. I'll hear the sound of her voice breaking in my sleep tonight. And the look on her face as she gathered up her things and left—I'll remember that forever. Someday, when Phoebe is back in the world of the living and all of this mess is behind me, I hope I can sit her down and explain it all to her. I hope she can forgive me.

I should feel elated. My plan worked. I am so much closer to reaching my sister. So why can't I stop crying?

Enough for tonight. The real work begins Monday, when we start rehearsals.

January 15

I could scream. I could break something. I was so close to her.

For days, I had been planning on slipping into the backstage on a ten-minute break, but every time, those silly McQueen boys wanted to walk with me to the fountain and continue discussing their "motivation" and "obstacles" in the scenes, or whatever. Dudes, it's a musical. Stand in your light and sing pretty. How hard is that?!

Today, though, there was an issue with a prop and Kevin McQueen went ballistic and stormed off, leaving the opening I was looking for. I found the stage door and it was PAD-LOCKED SHUT. What kind of Backstager locks the stage door with a padlock?! I tried to pick it, but some kid found me and started talking to me about feeding candy to a ghost or something, and then the break was over.

There was one stroke of luck, though. During the rehearsal, I started chatting up a Backstager named Aziz. I actually like him—he's the only one who seems to have his head in the game right now—but more importantly, I noticed he is the one who holds the key. I think I feel a new friendship blossoming . . .

⋈

January 16

Today is the day. I won't back down. Phoebe, your sister is coming to take you home.

CHAPTER 13

ND THAT'S WHEN I SAID, 'ORGANIC FOOD, MAN. IT GOES IN LOCAL and comes out express!' "

All of the actors howled at Aziz's story and he glowed, feeling for the first time what it was like to command an audience.

Rehearsal was wrapping up for the night, and for the first time, Aziz wasn't eating with one hand while building something with another. He was sitting down on the stage, socializing with the actors, of all people. Chloe was by his side, hanging on every word he said.

"Aziz, you are totally hilarious," she said. "Better not pick a comedy for the spring show, Kevin and Blake, or he may give you a run for your money!"

The McQueens smiled like Mona Lisa, unimpressed.

"Well, I'd better be heading back to my neck of the woods," she said, rising from the circle and gathering up a heavy black shoulder bag. "Aziz, don't make these guys laugh too hard—they have to save their voices for tomorrow!" And with that she was off, a shimmer of silver hair as she walked away from them toward the wings.

Aziz smiled. Could she be right? Could he actually be onstage, winning laughs like this nightly? Could he even be good enough to compete with the McQueens?

He loved being a Backstager, and he felt passionate about his work behind the scenes, but this feeling of being in the spotlight was pretty great, too. His glow diminished a bit, though, when out of the corner of his eye, he saw Jory, Sasha, and a winded-looking Beckett discussing something frantically. Beckett looked over at Aziz and they locked eyes. It was something serious.

"Excuse me, guys," Aziz said, rising to meet the group of Backstagers huddled in the wing.

※

"Beckett, that doesn't make any sense," Jory said.

"I know it doesn't, but here we are," Beckett replied, still gasping. He had sprinted all the way back from Bailey's house. His brain had not fully caught up to him.

"What's going on, guys?" Aziz asked.

"Oh, only that Chloe Murphy lied to get cast in the show," Beckett said. "She's not a current student at Penitent Angels."

"What? That's crazy. Why would she lie about that?" Aziz was totally baffled.

"Not only that," Beckett continued, "she was a Backstager at Penitent before she left."

"A Backstager?" Sasha was turning something over in his mind. "Well, that explains it!"

"Explains what, Sasha?" asked Jory.

"Why she was trying to get into the backstage. I found her tugging on the padlock."

"WHAT?" Beckett was a live wire again, even without the fuel of his Diet Coke. "Why didn't you tell anybody?"

"I was BUSY trying to talk to the GHOST," Sasha said. "And it's fine, because Aziz keeps the key safe."

"Right," Aziz said, confused, as he reached back for his key ring. Only it wasn't there. He looked up to the other Backstagers, the light draining from his eyes. He didn't even need to say it. They all knew.

"Come on," Beckett commanded, charging into the wings toward the stage door. Jory, Sasha, and a bewildered Aziz followed.

As they expected, when they reached the door, it stood ajar, the padlock hanging on its hinge. They ran down the stairs into the Club Room. To their terror, they found the Unsafe door standing open as well.

"I don't know what's going on," Beckett said. "But I have a BAD feeling."

Aziz grabbed a flashlight from a tool rack.

"Has anyone seen Hunter or the stage managers?" His mood was turning dark as the reality of Chloe's deception set in.

The rest of the Backstagers all shook their heads.

"Then we go in alone, because there isn't time to spare," Aziz said. "Everybody ready?"

One by one, the Backstagers slipped through the Unsafe door into the backstage.

The stars hanging above the tunnels were shining as beautifully as ever, but the boys were intent on finding the rogue Chloe. They opened each and every door they found, discovering mountains of props, pillars of speakers, an aviary of fluttering winged stage lights, a wardrobe packed with ball gowns enjoying their own ball, and a towering library of thousands of rows of scripts and scores—but no Chloe.

"It's too big," Jory said after shutting the door on the first-aid room, which was a fully functioning hospital of the highest order. "We're more likely to get lost in here forever than find her."

"We have to keep going," Aziz said, voice heated. "She tricked us deliberately to get back here. There must be a reason, and I seriously doubt it's to lend a hand with the *Phantasm* set."

"Okay, so what do we know about her?" Beckett said, trying to keep Aziz practical and not emotional.

"We know all the weird stuff started happening right before she showed up," Sasha said. "Do you think she knows the ghost?"

"Oh my gosh." Beckett turned a ghostly shade himself. "Bailey said Chloe dropped out of Penitent because there was a death in her family. Her little sister."

"You don't think . . ." Jory shuddered before he could even finish the sentence.

"I don't know," Beckett replied. "But doesn't it seem funny? The ghost light goes out, a light nearly *kills* Bailey, and suddenly this girl shows up and breaks into the backstage?"

"We've reached the end of the line, guys," Sasha said as the group reached the edge of a large chasm—a bottomless canyon cutting a dark edge into the backstage, like the end of the world. There, a bridge made piecewise from all manner of flats, props, signs, and other theatrical materials gripped the edge of the chasm and extended farther into the darkness. A sign scrawled above it read: PATCHWORK CATWALK.

"Not the *end* of the line," Aziz said ominously.

"Aziz, we can't," Jory said. "Even the stage managers don't cross the catwalk."

"I did once!" Sasha exclaimed. "I'll lead the way!"

"And do you remember what followed you back across?" Beckett asked sternly. Sasha's face fell.

"We may not have a choice, guys," Aziz said. "If she crossed the catwalk, then we have to go after her. Sasha, what do you remember about the other side?"

"It's just more tunnels, more doors."

"Just like here?"

"Well, the doors look . . . older. But yeah! It's not that scary!"

Aziz, Beckett, and Jory had a private conference, just with their eyes. Aziz nodded.

"Okay, Sasha," he said. "Lead the way."

Sasha nodded with an uncharacteristic maturity and started bravely across the catwalk. The others followed cautiously, pressing deeper into the dark.

When they reached the other side of the catwalk, they were met, as promised, with a line of heavier, more ancient-looking dark wooden doors, extending as far as they could see in either direction.

"What do we think?" Jory asked. "Left or right?"

"Either way, this could take hours, and I am getting seriously concerned that hours might equal days this deep in," Beckett said.

"Do we split up?" Aziz asked.

"Definitely not," Jory said.

"What if we just follow these tracks?" Sasha asked, pointing to the ground. The floor of this deeper and seemingly older part of the tunnels was covered in a layer of ashy soot, as if no feet had disturbed this ground in many, many years. Except one pair of feet had, as evidenced by a clear track of very fresh-looking sneaker prints veering off to the left, butting up against a few of the doors before trailing off into the dark.

"Good eye, Sash!" Aziz said, mussing Sasha's mop of blond hair. Sasha felt incredibly proud of himself. Sometimes, being so close to the ground had its advantages.

"She obviously tried a few of these doors and then went off looking for something," Jory said as the boys followed her trail.

"I wonder how she knows where to look for it," Beckett mused. "Bailey said she was only a Backstager for one semester—there's no way they took her this deep in."

"We're about to find out," Aziz said as the trail of footprints and the row of doors ended together at a larger, more ornate set of double doors at the end of the tunnel. One of its heavy wooden doors stood slightly ajar. The boys traded a look and stormed ahead. They went through the doors and into the darkness beyond.

For the first fifty paces or so, there was only black. Aziz shone his light around, but it only illuminated enough of the path in front of them to follow the sneaker prints. The rest of the space seemed limitless and completely empty.

As they pressed farther and farther into this blackness, each of them became a little less brave, so by the time they finally reached a towering black curtain dividing the empty darkness, no Backstager was prepared to actually walk through the curtain to see what was on the other side.

However, the footprints very clearly continued on, and so the Backstagers had to as well. Aziz lit the way while Jory pulled the curtain to one side, revealing a sight that filled all of them with a very particular dread.

Just beyond the curtain was a theater. They were onstage, looking into an empty house. It was not an overly ornate or particularly shabby theater. It wasn't monstrously huge or terribly intimate. It didn't look obviously creepy or dangerous. It looked, if you squinted, like pretty much any other theater, or *every* other theater you have ever seen, and that's why it was so frightening. The Backstagers recognized it immediately.

They had found their way back to the Arch Theater.

The Backstagers had been to the Arch Theater once before, and it had led to a world of trouble—their disappearance for two months; the disbanding of the Genesius Backstagers; the firing of their advisor, Mr. Rample; and very nearly their doom.

It was called the Arch Theater because it was the archetypal theater—the thing you thought about when you thought about theater as a concept. It was a place of tremendous power and danger, for it was the center of the whole backstage and possibly the heart of all theater magic. Time and space were nonlinear here. Literally anything was possible.

They had all vowed after the trouble earlier in the year that they would never return, but somehow it had found them. At the very least, they had also found Chloe, who was standing at the lip of the stage, staring at the Arch Theater's ghost light with wild eyes. She turned to greet her new audience of Backstagers.

"I guess I owe you an apology," she said, "or at least an explanation. I didn't mean to lure you guys down here—I was going to return the keys as soon as I was done, I promise."

"Why should we believe you?" Aziz asked, furious. "You tricked me. You lied to me!"

"But I didn't!" Chloe said. "I meant everything I said about you, Aziz."

"You were going to return the keys when you were done—done with what?" Jory asked.

"My mission," Chloe said. "The mission my sister gave to me."

"But isn't your sister . . . gone?" Beckett asked.

"For now, yes. But I found a way to speak with her." Chloe pulled the Spirit Board out of her bag. "She led me here. The closer I got to this place, the more clearly she spoke. I can feel her here. She's almost free. There's just this left in our way." She looked again at the ghost light hungrily, putting a hand on it.

"WAIT!" Jory said. "I really don't think you want to do that. Do you know what this place is?"

"I know it's where she's trapped," Chloe said. "And I know this is the way to get her back."

"Chloe," Aziz said, trying to maintain his composure,

"let's take a second to talk about this. Things aren't always what they seem here."

"MY INSTRUCTIONS WERE CLEAR!" Chloe shouted. "She told me herself. Now, I'm sorry I roped you all into this—that was not my intention. But now that you are here, you're not going to get in my way. This is my mission. My sister. MINE!"

She thrust the ghost light over, toppling it to the floor. The Backstagers all raced toward it, trying to break its fall, but they were too late. The bulb hit the stage and shattered with a great crash. All of the lights in the Arch Theater flickered out at once, plunging them into darkness. There was a terrible silence.

Chloe flicked on a flashlight from her bag, illuminating her face. Aziz's light flicked on, illuminating the Backstagers.

". . . Phoebe?" Chloe called into the darkness. The voice that replied was deep, otherworldly, and definitely not that of a little girl.

"NOT.   PHOEBE."

Wisps of blue and purple light began to coalesce from all directions on top of the spot where the ghost light had shattered. They swirled around one another, like trails of smoke from a just-blown-out candle, until they solidified into a towering, human-like form, equal parts light, smoke, and darkness. Two bloodred streaks of light slashed open where its eyes should be. The monster stood about ten feet tall, dwarfing Chloe and the Backstagers, who could only stare up at it in disbelief.

"YOU HAVE DONE WELL," it intoned. "THE GATE HAS BEEN OPENED."

"What . . . are you?" Beckett asked the beast.

A streak of red light appeared beneath its eyes, forming a devilish smirk.

"HUNGRY," it replied as it reached a smoky, spectral claw toward Chloe. Were it not for Aziz rushing to grab her arm and pull her toward the wings, she might have just let it take her, she was so frozen with fear, shock, and betrayal.

But she kept pace with all of them as they sprinted back through the curtain, through the dark expanse beyond, back through the double doors, back down the hall of doors, toward the Patchwork Catwalk.

Jory screamed for his life. Beckett managed to look back to see that the claw continued to reach for them, even after all their running, and had been joined by dozens more, groping after the fleeing kids with long, crooked fingers.

"I left candy for you at Genesius!" Sasha shouted back as he ran. "If you can wait five minutes, I'll bring it!"

"I don't think it wants candy, Sasha!" Aziz bounded toward the Patchwork Catwalk with all of his strength. "We're almost there! Hurry, guys!"

They raced across the rickety catwalk. It swayed and creaked under their combined weight. Aziz made the mistake of looking back and a claw caught up with him, catching his ankle and stopping him dead in his tracks as the others continued toward the other side of the canyon. He cried out as the other claws descended toward him. Sasha heard the call and doubled back to help his friend.

"I was NICE to you," he shouted at the claws, "and you are being a real JERK!" He wiggled around the trapped Aziz and stomped down hard on the ghost claw. It let out a hiss and retreated.

Sasha and Aziz narrowly ducked out of the way as the other fast-approaching claws just missed them, crashing into the catwalk, breaking gaping holes in its fabric. They looked at each other. Uh-oh.

Pieces of the catwalk began to come undone and fall all around them into the bottomless chasm below.

"GO!" Aziz shouted, and the two leaped across the quickly disintegrating pathway toward the others, who were waiting for them on the other side of the canyon.

With just a few yards to spare, Sasha and Aziz felt the full floor of the catwalk give way beneath their feet—they leaped for the edge and were airborne.

Something grabbed hold of Aziz and he screamed, sure that the ghost had managed to catch him again. He opened

his eyes and found that it was not more spectral claws, but Jory and Beckett, who were struggling to pull him the rest of the way up onto the ledge. Chloe and Sasha lent their strength, pulling at Jory's and Beckett's waists, and together they dragged Aziz to safety, landing in a big pile.

The last pieces of the Patchwork Catwalk fell impossibly far down into the blackness below. It was completely destroyed.

"Wow" was all Jory could say.

"Yeah," Beckett added.

"Um, guys," Sasha whimpered, pointing across the chasm.

Hundreds and hundreds of claws were suspended in the air. They shot upward across the chasm in an arc, raining down toward the kids like a volley of arrows in a medieval battle.

"Let's get out of here!" Beckett shouted as they surged back into the more familiar tunnels of the backstage, searching for the Unsafe door and the safety of the Club Room.

"This way!" Aziz shouted, noticing a familiar door and getting his bearings. He led the group around a tight corner as fifty shadowy claws shot forward down the hall they had just turned from, missing them by inches.

"There!" Beckett could see the Unsafe door up ahead. They raced through it, back into the Club Room, slamming the door shut behind them and throwing their backs against it, panting.

Chloe still couldn't speak. Aziz noticed for the first time that his ankle was bleeding. Jory slapped a hand on Beckett's shoulder, wordlessly acknowledging their teamwork in saving Aziz's life.

"Are we . . . okay?" Sasha asked.

"I don't know," Aziz said.

Their momentary peace was swiftly interrupted by a bang from the other side of the door. Chloe let out a scream, the first sound she had been able to produce since seeing the ghost. Another bang. The Backstagers put their full weight against the door.

Then they heard many fists pounding frantically. Jory looked to Beckett, terrified. Was this the end? Beckett shook his head, and then the door flung open, sending the Backstagers into a heap on the Club Room floor.

Hunter, Timothy, and Jamie crashed through the Unsafe door and landed on the pile.

"HUNTER," Jory gasped, pulling him into a hug.

Timothy leaped up and slammed the door shut, swiftly clicking its padlock closed.

"We were training in the backstage and everything went dark," he said, panting. "Then we saw some seriously spooky stuff. Is everyone all right? What were you guys doing back there unsupervised?!"

He took visual stock of his guys. Aziz, Sasha, Jory, Beckett, Hunter, and Jamie were all accounted for, if winded, scratched up, and seriously spooked. Then there was Chloe, crumpled on the floor, looking very close to tears.

"Chloe? What are you doing here?"

She looked up, guilt spreading across her face like a shadow.

"I have some explaining to do," she said as her first tears finally escaped, running down her cheeks, as silvery as her hair.

CHAPTER 14

EVERYONE WAS MAJORLY SHAKEN AS THEY GATHERED THEMSELVES in the Club Room for a Backstager emergency meeting. Jory and Hunter instinctively held hands as they sat down on the torn couch next to Aziz and Sasha. Beckett placed chairs for himself and Timothy and Jamie. For all the trauma they had just endured, they all felt slightly better just being together again. All except for their new guest, Chloe, who stood before the group, looking at the floor. She tried to speak and stammered, not sure where to begin.

"It's okay," Sasha said. "I was the one who messed everything up the last time and everyone was pretty cool about it. We know you didn't mean to."

She managed a weak smile at him and could finally make eye contact with the circle. She confessed the whole sad business—how she broke the Genesius ghost light herself, how she made contact with something she thought was her sister, how she dropped the light to startle Bailey Brentwood so that she could get the role of Crystalline, how she stole Aziz's keys to the backstage so that she could find the Arch Theater, and finally, she told them about the evil ghost she had awakened by shattering the Arch Theater's ghost light.

As she spoke, Timothy, Jamie, and Hunter listened carefully and without judgment. That is, until Jamie's phone was buzzing so consistently that he excused himself to see what the matter was.

"And so that's how we got here," Chloe concluded. "It was all my fault, and I am so, so sorry. I just . . . wanted her to be real so bad." Now she was crying heavy tears of guilt and embarrassment.

Timothy rose and poured her a paper cup of water from a cooler in the corner. "Thanks for coming clean," he said. "I know that wasn't easy. The good news is, we are all okay out here and that . . . thing . . . is stuck back there."

"I'm not so sure," said Jamie, who had returned to the Club Room, phone in hand and stricken expression on his face. "My phone is blowing up right now from Backstagers all over the country—heck, maybe all over the world. There's a new notification every minute—lights flickering in a theater in Dallas, soundboards crashing in Des Moines, props missing, sets failing, costumes tearing. All those little theater mishaps you write off as bad luck, but happening in every theater with a performance tonight, and at an alarming rate. Stage managers are asking if there is some colossal prank tonight they don't know about."

"I think I get it," Beckett said. "If the Arch Theater is the archetypal theater that powers all theater magic, then its ghost light must be the archetypal ghost light that powers all others."

"And its ghost is the archetypal ghost," Jory added. "That's why it was so huge and so powerful."

There was a collective shudder in the room as everyone considered the implications of that.

"It said the gate was open," Aziz whispered, understanding the gravity of what was going on. "When it materialized. Right before it grew a thousand arms and tried to snatch us all."

"If it can grow a thousand arms, maybe it could be that one ghost manifesting in all those theaters," Jamie suggested darkly.

"Why theaters?" Sasha asked.

"Theaters are liminal spaces," Chloe replied. It was all coming together in her mind.

"English, please?" said Aziz.

"Meaning they are boundaries—spaces between worlds.

I read about this in my research. Think about it—in a theater, the audience leaves the real world behind and enters a world of imagination that the writers and director and actors and Backstagers create for them. A world where magic is real—literally, it seems. That's why I chose a theater to try to contact my sister, and my guess is, that's why this . . . Arch Ghost . . . is materializing in theaters first. It's flexing its muscles with those little tricks, gaining power."

"Power for what?" Beckett asked.

"It said it was hungry," Aziz said, rubbing the freshly bandaged claw marks on his ankle.

"So we get back there and fix the ghost light," Hunter suggested.

"It's not so easy," Beckett said. "The first time we found the Arch Theater, we wandered into it totally by accident. Now we know a direct path, but it was across the Patchwork Catwalk, WHICH HAS NOW COLLAPSED. I have no idea how else to get back to the Arch Theater, and I don't think it is a very good idea to go wandering around the backstage looking for it when there are a thousand hungry ghost hands trying to snatch us up like we're finger food."

"What if we can get a good ghost to help us?" Sasha asked.

"Come on, Sash, this is serious," said Aziz.

"No, I mean it! Chloe summoned a bad ghost, but only

because she tried to summon a good ghost. If bad ghosts really exist, then good ghosts must really exist, too, like bad witches and good witches."

"But how do you suggest we find this good ghost?" Aziz asked.

"With a good *witch* . . ." Jory said, his wheels spinning.

"Jory, are you sure you didn't hit your head back there during the attack?" Hunter asked.

Jory jumped up, pulling out his phone. "I know someone who can help us!"

><

About an hour later, Reo was sitting with the group in the Club Room. Jory had attempted to quickly catch him up on the dire situation at hand, which also required he be caught up on the nature of the backstage, the Arch Theater, the tunnels, all of it. This turned into a sort of group reenactment as each Backstager chimed in with details he had missed or their own theories about how the backstage worked and what it all meant. Reo sat with his customarily stoic expression, a pale island in the dark sea of his robelike sweater and wide-brimmed hat.

"So THEN I got the idea to find a GOOD ghost, and Jory was like, 'I know a freaking WITCH!'" Sasha said, buttoning up the long tale with his arms outstretched to Reo. All of the Backstagers beamed at him expectantly.

Reo stood up and shouldered his bag.

"Hilarious," he said coldly. "You really played the long game with that one, Jory. For a minute there, I actually thought you wanted to be my friend. Now, if you've had your fun, I don't think I'm needed further." He started off toward the exit.

"Reo, wait!" Jory shouted. "It's all true, I promise!"

Reo spun around. "You know, I shared something really personal with you, Jory. It's not easy to open up to people. You've got to be a pretty terrible person to take that trust and make a joke out of it."

"Reo, I promise you! We don't have much time!"

As Jory pleaded with Reo to stay and the others looked around, unsure of what to do next, Sasha went over to the Unsafe door, turned the key still left in the lock, and slid the door open just a crack. He peeked in, checking for ghost claws, and when he saw none, he poked his whole head inside. Then his shoulders. Then he slipped completely into the backstage.

"And, Jory," Reo continued, his voice rising to a dramatic climax, "not that I would *ever* hex someone, I am not that kind of witch, but you should be SERIOUSLY careful about who you choose to—OHMYGOSHWHATISTHAT?!"

Reo's exit line was interrupted by a tiny, furry, four-legged purple monster galloping toward them, wagging its long turquoise tongue, its orange eyes glowing wildly. It leaped at Reo and tackled him to the floor as he screamed as if being devoured.

"That's FRIENDO! He LIKES YOU!" Sasha stood over Reo and the monster, beaming.

When Reo realized the monster wasn't actually devouring him but was licking him the way a puppy licks a friendly face, he jolted up, shaking Friendo off of him. The monster squealed and rushed under Sasha's legs, hiding.

"Oh look, now you've scared him!" Sasha said. He

reached into his pocket, producing a tiny little bowler hat. He placed it on the monster's head and it became calm, its long turquoise tongue dangling from the side of its mouth. Jory tiptoed up behind Reo, who was as stiff as a board, staring at the impossible furry creature staring back at him.

"It's called a tool mouse," Jory explained in a calming whisper. "One of the creatures who live back there. Totally harmless. Unless you're wearing red, in which case they can get a little overexcited."

"He's my BABY," Sasha said proudly as he scooped Friendo up and presented him to Reo once again. Friendo made something like a smile, quite pleased with his tiny hat.

Reo's face went from startled back to stoic. He drew a deep inhale, released it, and walked back to the circle of Backstagers. He took his seat and pulled his bag to his lap. He looked toward Jory, who shrugged as if to say, "And you thought your life was weird. " Reo smiled at last.

"Let's begin," he said.

CHAPTER 15

THEATER IS FULL OF RITUALS AND SUPERSTITIONS. EVEN BEFORE the McQueens ruled the St. Genesius Drama Club, the actors had a ritual of gathering in a circle onstage before every performance, holding hands, breathing together, and then jumping up and down ten times before breaking hands and screaming as loud as they could. No one knows who started it or why that was the prescribed good-luck ritual, but no one dared to begin a performance without doing it.

Now the Backstagers were making a circle of their own for a decidedly more old-school ritual. After calling all of their parents with a made-up sleepover scheme to buy them the night, Reo sent the group on a school-wide search for the items he required.

Jory borrowed some white chalk from a nearby class-room and drew out a circle on the stage floor big enough to seat all of them comfortably inside.

Aziz pulled every candle off of his prized candelabra set piece and arranged them neatly around the circle.

Hunter made sure there was a fire extinguisher nearby, because even though he was a ghost-whisperer tonight, he was a Backstager always, and safety came first.

Once the candles were all lit, Beckett lowered the stage lighting to black. For all of his love for electrics, he had to admit that the Genesius auditorium looked lovely in the candlelight.

Timothy raided the stage management fridge for a bottle of spring water. Reo had emphasized how it must be real spring water from the ground, and luckily, they were stocked.

Jamie searched and searched through their office pantry until he found what Reo had requested of him: sea salt—the real kind.

Always a devoted props master, Sasha brought an impressive array of options when Reo asked him for a cou-ple of bowls to hold the salt and the water and something fire-safe to burn some candles and incense on. There were brass goblets for a medieval magical feel, clay pots for a

more earthy vibe, minimalist plain white dishes for simple functionality, or glossy black varieties "because, witch." Reo told Sasha to choose whatever and Sasha agonized over this before deciding on a mix of all of them, just in case.

Chloe was lucky to already have on hand her requested item—a photo of her sister, Phoebe. She always kept one in her bag, and as she laid it in the center of the circle, she whispered a private apology to Phoebe for making such a mess of all of this.

Once everything was ready, the team sat cross-legged within the confines of the circle of chalk and candles. Reo mixed the salt into the water and walked clockwise around the circle, sprinkling the mixture along the perimeter.

"Let this be a circle of protection," he said. "Whatever evil spirit dwells in this space can do us no harm while we gather within it." The Backstagers held hands and bowed their heads, feeling safety in being together.

When he finished, Reo took his place at the top of the circle. Before him, he had arranged a little altar with Phoebe's photo, some incense from his bag, a glass of the spring water, a dish of the salt, and a black candle.

"You were right to try to talk to Phoebe here," Reo said to Chloe. "You just made some rookie mistakes and got the wrong number. That's the problem with those Spirit Boards. It's kind of like opening the front door to your house and letting whoever is walking by come in and hang out. And usually the spirits just wandering around looking for a place to go are not the kind you want to chill with. We're gonna make sure we get Phoebe on the line and once we do, we're gonna ask for her help—that make sense to everyone?"

He looked around the circle to each of the Backstagers and got an affirmative and brave nod from each.

"There's one last thing," Reo said, a bit of hesitancy in his voice. "I always thought of this stuff as something spiritual—something to give me confidence or peace or whatever. Like yoga but with more candles. I've read a lot about all of this, but I've never done anything quite like this tonight, and to be honest . . . I don't know if it will work. I don't really know if magic is real."

"Do you need me to get Friendo out again?!" Sasha asked. "Magic is as real as he is! It's as real as the ghost that's trying to take over the world. We believe in you, Reo!"

"I still have that moon power in me, and I definitely believe, Reo!" Jory agreed.

"We're so lucky you are here, Reo," Hunter said. "You're our best shot and so I believe."

"Me too," Aziz said. "I got a score to settle with that ghost!"

"Let's rock," Jamie said, proud of his team.

"Seconded," said Timothy, looking affectionately at Jamie. If nothing else, their relationship was full of adventure.

"Let's send this thing back to Dead Town," Beckett said as the candlelight flickering in his glasses made him look even more electrified than usual.

"And find the real Phoebe," Chloe said, gazing warmly at the photo of her smiling little sister.

For the first time in his entire life, Reo felt like part of a group. He felt powerful. It was actual magic.

"Thanks, guys," he said. "Let's toast this ghost."

He muttered a few quiet words over the black candle, salt, water, and incense before turning his attention to the photo of Phoebe.

"Tonight," he announced to the air, "we wish to speak to Phoebe Murphy and only to Phoebe Murphy. Phoebe, your sister tells me you loved performing onstage and so we have prepared a stage just for you tonight to come visit us and lend us some help. Your sister is here and she would love to speak to you!"

Just then, a gentle draft blew across the stage, making the candles flicker. Jory raised his eyes to Reo. Something was happening.

"Everyone look at the photo," Reo told the group. "Focus with everything you've got on reaching Phoebe. We need to all hold that intention in our minds together."

Across the stage, in the stage right wing, a broom propped up by the stage management calling desk started to wobble. It rose up slightly into the air. Then it fell to the ground with a slam. Sasha looked up at the noise and noticed the broom slithering across the floor like a pale snake, straight for the circle.

"Uh, guys . . ." he whispered.

"Focus!" Reo ordered.

The broom kicked up into the air, its handle pointed at Reo like a dart.

"GUYS!" Sasha warned. They all looked up from the photo just in time to see the broom launch toward Reo at a terrifying velocity. Reo flinched, bracing for impact, but when the handle of the broom reached the edge of their circle of candles and chalk, it splintered into pieces and fell as if it had slammed into an invisible brick wall.

"It's working! The circle is working!" Reo cried, more surprised than anyone that his spell held actual power.

"And that thing is getting angry," Aziz cautioned.

"We have to hurry," Reo said. "Chloe, talk to your sister. Let her know it's you calling. Talk about things only she would know."

Chloe nodded and focused on the photo of her sister. It was a photo she had taken on the day Phoebe had decided to buzz her hair. The medicine was going to make it fall out, but Phoebe didn't want to wait. Losing her hair was part of the treatment process, and Phoebe had been a warrior all along. Still, some dragons can't be slain by even the mightiest warriors, and Phoebe lost her battle. She looked quite different before she passed away, but Chloe would always remember her like this: her curls pulled up into her signature pom-poms, her eyes alight with bravery and determination.

"Phoebe, it's me, Chloe. I'm here today because we need your help. I ended up making a big mess of things because I lied and tricked a lot of people, but it was only because I was trying to get to you. I've missed you so much."

As Chloe petitioned her sister, the scraps of the broom rose and started to shoot toward the barrier of the magic circle again and again, like pouring rain against a window. Piles of lumber stacked here and there for building sets rose and joined the onslaught. Then a full table of props. Then a box of nails. Those in the circle could only watch, terrified, as the protective dome created by the magic circle was pummeled from every angle by seemingly every piece of debris in the theater.

"It's getting stronger!" Jory shouted.

"Keep your focus, everyone!" Reo held his stare at Phoebe's photo, but he looked truly scared as all manner of theater-making material crashed into the invisible wall just behind and above his head.

"It's all my fault, as usual," Chloe continued, pitching her voice over the rain of objects darting against the barrier. "Just like that time I wanted to dress up like mermaids and I stuck the jewels all over us with actual glue. Do you remember that? Mom and Dad were so mad, but we looked amazing!" She laughed, in spite of the escalating crashing all around them. "Or the time I wanted to take us to meet that singer at that faraway mall and got us on the wrong bus. We were so lost and I just couldn't stop crying, but you were so brave and resourceful. You stayed calm and asked directions and got us to the right mall in time to get that autograph and all the way home, safe and sound."

The enormous candelabra set piece began to shake and rise, defying gravity as it floated into the air and dangled above the protective dome of the magic circle. It spun there, threatening to drop at any moment. Reo began to quietly chant, "Phoebe. Phoebe. Phoebe." The others joined him, a rhythmic call underneath Chloe's plea.

"That was you in every situation. Even when you were sick, you were the one comforting me, and now that you're gone, I don't have anyone to be brave for me. So I tried to be brave myself, and it turned out like this. So please, Phoebe, come back and bail me out one more time. I need you— but more than that, I just want to see you again because I miss you! I miss you so much! And I love you, Phoebe! I LOVE YOU!"

Chloe's last cry rang out and filled the theater as all of the candles blew out at once and the enormous candelabra came crashing down into the blackness.

CHAPTER 16

JORY OPENED HIS EYES SLOWLY. EVEN THAT SMALL ACTION SEEMED TO take the effort of lifting a car. His vision was blurry, but he began to get his bearings.

The auditorium was a total wreck. There was debris everywhere, but now instead of flying through the air, it all lay lifeless on the stage floor. There was something else lying lifeless among it. Jory blinked a few times as a shocking sight came into focus—it was Jory himself. He was buried among the rubble, eerily still. Jory stared at himself, trying to figure out exactly what he was seeing, when he heard a gasp. It was Sasha, trying to lift a piece of wood that had pinned another, inert, Sasha. As the dust settled around him, Jory could see all of his friends struggling to free themselves from the rubble.

"Is everyone okay?" Reo asked, gliding into the center of the space.

"Most definitely NOT, dude!" Beckett replied, pulling on his own arm. "Why am I outside of my body?!"

"We all are!" Aziz cried, staring at his own body just below him.

"Yeah," Reo said, forlorn. "I think . . . we died."

"WHAT?" Sasha shouted. "If I died, my mom will KILL ME."

"But why are we still here?" Hunter asked, drifting into focus.

"Unfinished business," Chloe said, her silver hair flowing around her as if she were underwater. "Guys, I think we're ghosts."

"This . . . this is impossible," Jamie said as he examined his own hands.

"So is flying, but we're all doing it," Reo said.

Looking down, the Backstagers noticed that they weren't standing on the ground above their bodies, but were actually floating a few inches off the stage. They also began to realize for the first time that while the bodies on the ground were fleshy and solid, their new forms were more like smoke or gauze—indistinct and fluid.

"I'm really sorry," Reo said. "I failed us."

Jory shook his head. "You did your best. We wouldn't have made it as far as we did without you."

"And if our goal was to find a good ghost," Sasha explained, "we actually have EIGHT good ghosts now!"

"He's right," Hunter said. "We're still here for a reason. We may not have made it out alive, but this thing is bigger than us, and what kind of Backstagers would we be if we didn't keep fighting, even if it kills us? Even AFTER it kills us?"

"Genesius Backstagers never quit," Timothy replied. "I'm in."

"Same here," said Jamie. "We're all ghosts, but we're all together."

"And if we're already dead, then we can't lose, can we?" asked Aziz.

"And, guys," Jory said, pointing across the auditorium, "I think we better hurry."

A shadowy slice hung there above the orchestra seats: a rip through the fabric of reality. Two ghost claws protruded through the crack, trying to pull it apart from either side. As the crack widened, they could see the red eyes of the Arch Ghost gleaming hungrily from the darkness beyond.

"It's about to break through!" cried Beckett.

"Not while I'm haunting this theater," Chloe said as she flew up into the air in an impossibly cool, action-movie kick and slammed her sneaker into one of the spindly ghost fingers. The Arch Ghost hissed from the other side of the crack.

"Oh, no you don't!" Beckett cried as he picked up a broken piece of cable from the rubble and cracked it like a whip at another ghost finger. The finger recoiled back into the portal.

The ghostly Backstagers all shared a look—they knew what they had to do. At once, they charged toward the lip of the stage, leaped, and took flight toward the portal like a pack of superheroes armed with two-by-fours, prop torches, music stands, and power drills. When they made impact with the portal, they completely overpowered the Arch Ghost, sending it screaming deep into the dimension from whence it came.

Unfortunately, they also overpowered the portal itself, and it tore further open and swallowed the lot of them up as if they were a team of sledding dogs crashing through thin ice. They plummeted out of their own dimension into that of the Arch Ghost before the portal snapped closed again, trapping them in that alternate world and plunging the Genesius auditorium into darkness.

When they landed on the other side of the portal, the Backstagers found themselves on the stage of the Arch Theater, at the gaping mouth of an injured and furious Arch Ghost.

"YOU THINK BREAKING MY FINGERS WILL STOP ME?" it roared as a hundred new claws grew from its back. It flexed its thousand new razor-sharp fingers. "YOU ARE IN MY DOMAIN NOW, WHERE I AM AT FULL POWER. WHAT MAKES YOU THINK YOU CAN DEFEAT ME, THE FIRST GHOST, WHO RULES ALL OTHERS?"

"You think this is your domain?" Timothy asked with a laugh. "You're in the theater now, and you're messing with the best Backstagers in the business."

"And don't forget, you killed us and we are still here fighting you," Aziz said defiantly. "From where I'm standing, it looks like we have nothing left to lose."

"YES, I'VE ALREADY CLAIMED YOUR BODIES. NOW I SHALL CLAIM YOUR SOULS!"

Jory winced at this, but he knew they had reached the point of no return.

"Everyone at places?" Jamie shouted, swinging his intercom pack around on its wire like a medieval weapon. "Then let's go!"

They charged the Arch Ghost as it thrust its hundred claws toward them.

Aziz had picked up a plank of wood that he deftly swung, bludgeoning claw after claw away.

Jory had a bolt of fabric that he twirled about, shielding and deflecting the groping claws like a bullfighter. Out of the corner of his eye, he saw a claw dive for Hunter, who was using his fire extinguisher to blast each attack away. Jory leaped into the path of the reaching fingers and swatted them away. Hunter shot Jory a grateful wink and continued the battle.

Jamie was particularly adept with his intercom pack, swinging and bashing away claws at impressive distances. Later, Timothy would remember to swoon over his boyfriend-turned-action-hero, but for now, he was busy dodging strikes and trying to think of a plan.

Reo tossed his wide-brimmed hat like a boomerang. As it soared about the theater, it took out several claws in one graceful strike before returning to its owner. It was a move Reo had daydreamed when he drew himself as an anime superhero but couldn't imagine actually pulling off. In the spirit world, it seemed that thought and belief mattered more than what was actually possible in the regular world.

Sasha came barreling toward the Arch Ghost at incredible speed armed with his prop torch. He batted a few descending claws aside with its handle, but when he switched the flame on, the arms of the Arch Ghost seemed to fizzle and dissolve around him.

"The light!" he shouted to his comrades. "It hates the LIGHT!"

Timothy looked up from a ghostly wrist he was strangling to see that Sasha was right.

"Beckett! Chloe!" he shouted. "You're our electrics kids. Fix that ghost light, fast! We'll fight him off!"

Beckett turned to Chloe and she shouted an affirmative "Copy!"

As the others fought off the Arch Ghost's army of claws, Beckett and Chloe darted into the wings to make a quick plan.

"I'll take stage left, you take stage right," Chloe whispered. "There's got to be a replacement bulb in here somewhere. Once we find it, it's a simple install job."

"Give a shout if you find it. And be careful. This place has a mind of its own," Beckett replied.

They split up and began searching. The wings of the Arch Theater were full of mysterious artifacts. Boxes and boxes of ancient-looking goblets, daggers, candles, and shields may have been props or may have been actual antiques from some lost civilizations—there was no way to know for sure.

Chloe frantically dug through a rack of containers that seemed to hold every kind of theatrical light, from the flame and mirror setups of antiquity up to the most modern intelligent lamps. Unfortunately, no lightbulbs. She thought she was at least in the right department, but when she examined the next rack, all of its containers had Greek masks, stone faces elaborately expressing comedy or tragedy. Confused, she returned to the previous rack to see if she had missed something, but now the containers no longer held theater lights—they were full of ropes and wires. The Arch Theater was toying with her.

Meanwhile, onstage, the other Backstagers were struggling to deal with the attacks of the Arch Ghost. As soon as they defeated one wave of its talons, another would appear. The Arch Ghost seemed to have limitless power, and the Backstagers, even in their elevated spirit form, were getting tired.

Hunter had just blasted away a shadowy hand when he saw yet another approaching. He pointed his extinguisher and fired, but no juice was left to drive the hand away. The talon grabbed the tool from Hunter and cast it away into the darkness.

Hunter looked around for something—anything— to defend himself with, but before he could act, he was snatched up by the giant claw and hoisted into the air. Jory could only watch from afar, busy as he was fighting off his own attackers, as Hunter was pulled into the belly of the Arch Ghost, disappearing into its shadowy blackness.

"Hunter, NO!" Jory cried as he threw down his fabric shield and sprinted with full force toward the Arch Ghost. He dove after Hunter into the Arch Ghost's massive form, vanishing into the dark.

Timothy and Jamie were back to back, both fighting off the claws and defending each other. Jamie swung his intercom pack into at least a dozen foes before the Arch Ghost learned his strategy and caught the pack like a baseball. Jamie's eyes widened as the claw then tugged the pack, wire, and Jamie along with it up into the air. Timothy turned just in time to grab Jamie's sneaker and start a tug-of-war with the ghost. The match was a short one, however, as more claws quickly swept Timothy up by the ankles and carried them both into the black belly of the Arch Ghost.

The ghost seemed to grow in size and power as it overtook each Backstager. Soon, the remaining warriors didn't stand a chance.

Sasha cowered beneath his torch, which provided a thin barrier of protection. The Arch Ghost reached for him, but its arms dissolved again and again as they hit the light. This was a clever ghost, though, and it managed to snatch Sasha up by plunging a claw into the stage floor and grasping up beneath him. Sasha was so startled when he felt the cold, sharp fingers wrap around his tiny leg that he dropped the torch, extinguishing its light and leaving him defenseless against his attacker. He was soon pulled in with the others.

Reo took out throngs of the claws before the ghost got wise and caught his hat. Reo had another trick up his sleeves—literally. When the claws rained back down upon him, he tossed a handful of something he had been concealing in his sweater—the sea salt left over from their magic circle.

The grains of salt hit the shadowy hands like acid rain, turning them instantly to dust. His plan bought him enough time to look around and notice that he was the last Backstager standing. He also noticed for the first time how the Arch Ghost had grown impossibly tall, filling the entire Arch Theater with shadow. It smiled a sinister red smile at Reo as a thousand new claws filled the air around it. Reo slowed his breathing and pulled out a silver chain hanging around his neck, revealing a silver star necklace that had been hiding beneath his shirt. It was a pentagram, the five-pointed star of protection. He held it tightly and closed his eyes as the claws descended all around him.

In the wings, Beckett rummaged through crate after crate of theatrical bric-a-brac, searching for the bulb. Like Chloe, he had quickly discovered that the boxes would change their contents as soon as their lids were replaced, so rather than moving between boxes, Beckett now searched one single crate over and over again. First it was mic belts, then it was scripts, then it was thread, then it was makeup. Every time he replaced the lid and pulled it off again, a new heaping pile of equipment appeared before him. Eventually, he stopped searching through the piles at all but could just judge at a glance if he was even looking at lighting department stuff.

He lifted and dropped the lid again and again as if he were clicking through slides on a projector: curtains, plywood, power tools, pointe shoes, coffee, gaff tape, lightbulbs. LIGHTBULBS! He stopped and threw the lid aside, rummaging through the bulbs. There were colorful fairy lights, twisty eco bulbs, tiny desk bulbs, antique Edison bulbs, and—at last!—a large plain white filament bulb—exactly right for a ghost light.

"Guys! I got it!" Beckett shouted.

He was met with an eerie silence.

"Guys?"

He saw his breath plume out in front of him as the temperature suddenly dropped to below freezing. Beckett turned slowly. At his back were a dozen outstretched ghost hands, hanging silently in the air, ready to pounce. Beckett screamed as they shot down at him, swallowing him up and shattering the bulb on the stage floor.

Chloe was completely lost. She had followed a rack of crates far into the wing, checking each for the bulbs to no avail. When she looked back, she couldn't see the stage but only an endless row of crates extending into nothingness. She looked in the direction she had been heading and saw the same. Somehow, she had entered a deeper part of the Arch Theater that had lost the form of a functional stage and was now just the idea of storage—storage as far as the eye could see or the mind could comprehend.

She had no idea how to return, but she figured she would worry about that when she found the bulb. She opened more crates. Chalk. Cough drops. Fog machines. Water bottles. Staff paper. Pencils. Each new box mocked her. She was getting frustrated. Granola bars. Staples. Rope. Pencils again. She crumpled on the ground in tears.

"SHOW ME WHAT I'M LOOKING FOR!" she shouted to no one.

She couldn't hold back anymore and sobbed. She had made such a terrible mess of everything. She'd literally gotten a bunch of people killed and possibly put the world in danger from a force she was not nearly strong enough or smart enough to combat.

After a few heavy sobs, she started to collect herself, but the sounds of her crying still echoed around the space. She sat upright, confused.

Now she wasn't crying at all but could hear the unmistakable sound of a girl in tears. It was near.

She looked through a few boxes. More theater stuff, but no tears. She zeroed in on the sound a few boxes away. She looked inside—only sandbags. She pulled the box out from the rack and found behind it a little girl, maybe about nine years old, cowering in the dark. Her curly hair, pulled into pom-poms, obscured her face.

"Phoebe?" Chloe gasped.

CHAPTER 17

'M SCARED."

"Me too."

"I'm lost."

"Me too. But it's me, Chloe."

"Who?"

"Don't you remember, silly? Your sister, Chloe."

". . . Chloe."

"Yes."

"I think . . ."

"Yes?"

"I think I remember."

"Good! I remember you. I miss you."

"I don't remember me."

"No?"

"Not really."

"Your name is Phoebe."

"Oh . . . Yes."

"You are nine years old and you love acting onstage very much and your sister loves you very much."

"Onstage."

"Yes."

"Is that where we are now?"

"No, we're backstage, somewhere."

"I don't like it here."

"Me neither."

"How did I get here?"

"Well, you left us, your family. You left us behind. And maybe you got lost? Trying to find your way back onstage, I bet."

"I left?! I'm sorry."

"No, don't be sorry. You didn't have a choice. You couldn't stay anymore. We were all so sad."

"I'm sorry."

"Don't be."

"I don't understand why I would leave. I don't like being alone."

"You're not alone. Not anymore."

"No."

"Because your sister is here now."

"Chloe."

"Yes."

"I . . . I remember."

"Yes? What do you remember?"

"I remember a tree . . . and a slope . . . white . . . cold."

"And a sled?"

"Yes!"

"Yes, sledding in the backyard. School was canceled for ·
the day and the day seemed to last a year."

"Yes! We rode the sled down the hill by the tall tree.
Over and over. And then . . . someone called."

"Mom?"

"MOM! Yes. Mom. I remember."

"And she made us hot cocoa and all the snow was still
stuck in your hair when we came inside, into the warm."

"Yes! I was feeling better that day."

"You were."

"Yes. I was feeling much better. It was a few weeks
before we found out . . . oh."

"But before that! Before that time! What do you
remember?"

"And then I wasn't feeling better anymore. I just felt
worse and worse . . ."

"Phoebe, hey! Stay with me! Before all of that, can you
remember anything else? Can you remember your dance
recital?"

". . . Dance?"

"This was a year or so before the snow day. You were making your debut onstage, dancing. At Penitent Angels, remember?"

". . . I . . . I don't know."

"Mom and Dad were bickering because Dad made us late picking out a tie and Mom was like, 'All of your ties are the same,' and he was like, 'Not when my daughter is performing onstage. I need to look my best,' and Mom was like, 'To look your best, we need a time machine,' and we all laughed so hard."

"Yes! Time machine, yes!"

"And you went and danced and we watched and applauded and you were so amazing and then we all went to dinner and you got to pick the place. Do you remember what you picked? Phoebe? Can you remember?"

". . . Pizza?"

"Of COURSE you did! Every chance you got!"

"I remember!"

"What do you remember?"

"At the pizza place, Mom said that we'd had enough and it was late and Dad said, 'We've had enough when Phoebe says we've had enough,' and Mom said—"

"'You're right.' I remember, too."

"And we ate so much."

"SO much."

"I miss that."

"I miss it too, Phoebe."

"I miss everything. Cold and warm and hungry and full and dancing and Mom and Dad—"

"I miss you."

"I miss you, too. And life. I miss life."

"Life misses you, Phoebe."

"Really?"

"So much. It's not the same. Not even close. That's why I came all the way here. I wanted to try to find you and bring you back. Back to life. Because it hasn't been life without you in it."

"But to get here—how did you get here?"

"I died, too, Phoebe."

"No! That's too far, Chloe."

"I know. I made a mistake. And I got a lot of people hurt."

"Can we fix it?"

"I don't know."

"Can we try?"

"I don't know."

"Of course we can. We can always try. We might fail, but if we don't try, we failed already."

"That's you, Phoebe! That's my sister. I always loved your attitude. Oh!"

"What, Chloe?"

"When I took your hand just now, as soon as we touched—look! We're glowing!"

"We are? Oh! We are."

"We're glowing, Phoebe! Like stars!"

"Like fireflies!"

"Like candles!"

"Like magic jewel-covered mermaids!"

"You remember!"

"I remember!"

"We're brighter now, Phoebe."

"I can see the way now—the way back."

"Yes, we're lighting the way!"

"Let's hurry. Don't let go of my hand, Chloe."

"I won't. I won't ever."

"Here, this way! Oh."

"WHO GOES THERE?"

"I am Phoebe Murphy and this is my sister, Chloe Murphy. Who are you?"

"WHO AM I? I AM THE END OF THE DARK ROAD. I AM THE FINALITY. I AM THE SHADOW."

"Phoebe, I'm so scared."

"Don't be scared, I'll protect you."

"I AM THE LAST CURTAIN."

"Okay! We get it!"

"Phoebe!"

"It's okay, Chloe, I'm not scared of it. I've been to the end of the road. I've gone into the shadow. I watched the curtain fall. None of it could drown out this light!"

"Phoebe, we're getting brighter!"

"My sister crossed the barrier between life and death to find me and help me remember. And I do remember! Our love survived your shadow and it always will!"

"It's filling the theater! Like the sun!"

"IT BURNS! IT BURNS!"

"Now begone, you cold, creepy thing! You aren't welcome here. Chloe is a Backstager and I am an Onstager and you are a guest in this house! And you aren't WELCOME HERE!"

"IT   B U R N S!"

⋊⋉

You know when a big musical number or a particularly dramatic scene ends in a quick blackout? Think of the opposite.

CHAPTER 18

CHLOE OPENED HER EYES. THE ARCH THEATER WAS ALIGHT WITH A beautiful amber glow as all of its lanterns, footlights, sconces, and hanging lamps hummed back to life. She still held Phoebe's hand tightly, but when she looked over to her sister, she saw that she had transformed somehow. Phoebe hovered just above the stage, a luminous halo shining around her. She held the broken ghost light like a scepter and appeared very much like a fairy queen.

"We did it," Chloe whispered.

"Yes," Phoebe said. Even though she was still in her nine-year-old body, she spoke with a grace and serenity far beyond her years. It was as if she had grown into an adult in those few luminous moments when her light engulfed and defeated the Arch Ghost.

"Let's fix the light, fast, and get back to Genesius!" Chloe started to head toward the wing and the cases of equipment.

"Chloe, I can't go back with you."

"What? Why?"

"You could fix the light, sure, but then someone could break it again and the Arch Ghost would return. It was the light inside of me, the light of our love that defeated it this time. And that light is eternal."

"What are you saying?"

"I'm saying I will stay here and guard the door. I will become the ghost light."

"Forever?!"

"Forever is a long time, yes, but look at this place. Can you imagine a better place to spend eternity than on a stage like this, at the heart of everything that makes theater magical?"

Chloe looked around. In this light, the Arch Theater looked regal and gorgeous. Peaceful, even. A tear rolled down her ghostly cheek.

"But what will I do without you?" Chloe asked. "It's been so hard."

"Don't you see, Chloe? I'll be right here, protecting every show you ever work on. Even if you never return to the Arch Theater, you can find me in any ghost light in any theater you set foot in. I'll always be with you."

"Okay," Chloe said, wiping her tears. "I guess this is goodbye, for now."

"For now," Phoebe said, smiling. "I can't wait to see all the great things you do."

"Thanks, sis. I'll do my best."

"You should get back to your friends now."

"Where is everyone?"

"I lit their way home. I'll light yours, too." Phoebe raised her ghost light scepter into the air, and the light from her glowing halo began to gather where its bulb had been. The ball of light grew brighter and brighter.

Chloe shielded her eyes as the light became blinding, and then she was falling. She plummeted down and down, what felt like miles, until she slowed and landed, quite gently, back in her own body. She opened her eyes and gasped for air as the circle of Backstagers surrounding her let out a cheer.

"Better late than never!" Beckett shouted, gripping his chest in relief.

"Yeah, we thought you were dead for REAL," Sasha said, beaming.

"We were all dead for real," said Aziz, brushing sawdust from his sweater. "But I feel surprisingly okay. Not even a headache."

"What . . . what happened?" Chloe asked as she tried to rise to her feet.

"Take it easy now," Timothy warned, swooping in to help her up. "It took us all a second to get fully . . . back."

"That thing gobbled us all up," Jamie said as he brought Chloe a paper cup of water. "It was pretty dark and awful in there—like the saddest, darkest days of your life all mashed up into one feeling. But then there was this light, this totally . . . beautiful light. And then we all woke up here."

"Except for you," Jory said. "So we were worried."

"It was Phoebe," Chloe told them. "She saved us. She saved everybody. She's the light inside the ghost light."

They all turned to look at Genesius's own ghost light emitting a friendly glow at the lip of the stage.

"Thank you, Phoebe," Hunter said to the light. "I would have loved to meet you, but we are all so grateful."

The Backstagers all nodded and whispered their own thanks to the light. Chloe could feel her sister's presence and knew she could hear them.

"What time is it?" Reo asked, clearly feeling the fatigue of a long night spent battling across life and death.

"Almost five!" Timothy replied. "I bet the sun is coming up."

"What do we do now?" Sasha asked, yawning.

"Look at this place!" Jamie said, surveying the rubble all around them. "We get to work cleaning this up before rehearsal tonight! We have a show to do!"

Everyone smiled and nodded, grateful to be alive and excited to be Backstagers again.

CHAPTER 19

WHAT DO YOU MEAN SHE CAN'T PLAY THE ROLE?! WE ARE WEEKS deep into rehearsal!"

Kevin McQueen was, understandably, not taking the news about Chloe Murphy's departure from *Phantasm* well.

"It's the rules, Kevin, I'm sorry," Timothy replied. "The guest actress has to be a current student at Penitent Angels, and Chloe lied."

"Well, CHANGE THE RULES," roared Blake. "She's the only Crystalline we could find!"

"We are holding an emergency work session tonight for Bailey Brentwood," said Jamie. "She's been working on the material and wants another shot. This time with no spooky, near-death surprises."

The McQueens took a simultaneous deep breath.

"Fine," Kevin snorted. "If anyone can catch up, it's Bailey, but if she doesn't have that high note—"

"Let's just see what she's got," said Timothy.

In the wing, Beckett was once again a sweaty mess. This was equal parts due to the fact that he had kept himself awake all day drinking more Diet Cokes than he ever had before, and the fact that Bailey's second chance was moments away. As he stood there sweating and spinning, a dark figure crept up behind him surreptitiously. It dropped a pale hand onto his shoulder and Beckett nearly jumped out of his body once again. He turned to the figure and let out a sigh.

"Reo, you scared me half *back* to death!" he whispered.

"Sorry, I'm not used to having friends. I gotta learn how to, like, approach," Reo said.

"Did you bring it?" Beckett asked.

"Of course, my man," Reo replied, pulling a necklace from his pocket. It was an orange stone dangling from a silver chain.

"I owe you, dude!" Beckett said.

"Ah please, it's the least I can do. We're a coven now!"

"Got anything for my nerves?"

"I could probably whip something up, but honestly, Beck, the magic is you. You've got this."

Beckett nodded and closed his hand around the necklace, determined.

⋇

In the opposite wing, Bailey was doing a breath exercise to center herself. The call about the replacement audition had come in just a few hours ago and she didn't have nearly as much time to prepare as she would have liked, but this was a second chance and she was going to give it everything she had. Beckett tiptoed up to her.

"Hey," he said gently. "Sorry, I didn't mean to interrupt, I just wanted to catch you before you went out there."

"Beckett! Hey, no worries, I was hoping to run into you. Can you believe this? I hope I didn't, like, snitch on Chloe. It was so not my intention to get her kicked out—"

"No, no way, she came clean on her own. She felt really bad about the whole thing. She's just been having a hard time since she left Penitent and wanted an outlet."

"Of course. Well, I hope she's okay."

"I have a feeling she is."

"So are all the lights secure this time? Or should I warm up my legs to dodge out of the way?"

Beckett laughed, embarrassed. "I literally triple-checked."

"I like those odds."

They stood there a moment in contented silence.

"Hey, so I got you something," Beckett said. He held out the necklace and put it in Bailey's palm.

"Oh Beck, it's gorgeous!"

"It's a citrine. The stone. It's supposed to give you confidence. Not that you need it. You're gonna kill it out there."

"Trust me, I'll take all the help I can get! Thank you, Beckett. That's super thoughtful."

"Of course! And one more thing . . ." Beckett's words caught in his throat. "Can I actually borrow that back for one sec?" Bailey handed him back the necklace and Beckett clutched the stone, trying to grasp that bit of confidence he needed to say what he wanted to say next.

"No matter what happens, I'd love to see you more. Like, obviously I miss hanging like we used to at Penitent and I'd love any opportunity to see you more, but lately, to be honest, I've actually been wondering, if it wouldn't be totally weird or like ruin our friendship or anything, if we maybe tried, just like once, just to see, tried going out for like—"

"A date?" Bailey asked with a chuckle. She didn't chuckle because the idea was preposterous; she chuckled because Beckett was so adorably frazzled. His baseline energy was a bit frazzled, but this was supercharged. "Beckett, you're not making a great case for the effectiveness of that magic charm. If you're gonna ask me, ask me!"

Beckett sighed and laughed at himself. Then, feeling a surge of confidence that may have come from the necklace, the caffeine pulsing through him, or just that gut feeling when you know something is right, he looked Bailey Brentwood, the Coolest Girl in the World, right in the eye and asked, "Do you wanna go on a date sometime?"

"Yeah," she said, trying to keep her growing smile casual. "Yeah, I think that could be cool."

"Okay," Beckett said as the reality of the moment began to spread across his face. "Cool."

"Cool," she repeated. They both laughed again. "Well, I better get myself focused."

"Yeah! Yeah, totally." He handed her back the necklace. "Break a leg."

"Thanks, Beckett."

As he walked away, he thought that all of the Diet Coke in the world couldn't give him this kind of buzz.

Aziz sat in the auditorium, exhausted from the full day of rebuilding but also feeling a bit low. He forgave Chloe for lying to him and understood why she did it, but he also felt embarrassed for actually thinking she saw something special in him. He had felt so *seen* when he was improvising with the actors, but it was just a ploy. Now Chloe was gone and he was just another crew guy again. He knew that this was probably all he was cut out for, but it was hard to come back to reality after letting himself dream of being more.

"THERE you are!" Aziz turned to see Jamie's fuzzy grin. "Mind if I join you?"

"Sure thing," Aziz said. Jamie plopped down in the seat next to him. They looked up at the set.

"Man, I can't believe we got all that done," Jamie said. "Nothing like saving the world AND a major theatrical production in the same all-nighter and having no one ever know about it."

"Ha. Yeah."

"But that's being a Backstager, isn't it? Everyone just sees the secret identity, not the superhero."

"I guess it is."

"But I want you to know that I see the superhero. All us Backstagers do. Especially Sasha. He looks up to you most of all. Today at dinner break, he told Jamie and me all about how you've been picking up everyone's slack around here while we were training Hunter. Building that candelabra, running lights, fetching props. That's majorly impressive, dude! It's future stage manager material."

The light came back on in Aziz's eyes. He tried to play it cool.

"But Hunter can talk to you about that next year when you're a junior and ready to take the trials yourself."

Jamie patted Aziz on the shoulder before getting up and heading off to other duties. A smile spread across Aziz's face.

Sasha, who had been watching the whole scene from behind a set piece, lit up when he saw that smile. He unzipped his jacket slightly and whispered to the fuzzy secret he was hiding within, "I FIXED something! I FIXED SOMETHING!"

Friendo purred in approval against Sasha's chest.

Back in the Club Room, Jory and Hunter were still deep in a perfect nap on the couch. An alarm on Jory's phone wrenched them back to life.

"Noooooooo," Jory croaked.

"I know." Hunter yawned. "Time for rehearsal."

"Five more minutes?" Jory asked.

"They do need to do Bailey's audition. I think we're safe."

The boys leaned back on the couch.

"This is nice," Jory said.

"Yeah."

"I missed you."

"Me too." Hunter sat up. "Can this break be over, Jory? I thought I would be more focused without you as my boy-friend, but I wasn't at all. I can't help it. I have a serious Jory addiction."

"I know what you mean." Jory chuckled. "But it was important, I think. It was scary to get out on my own, but I made friends with Reo and look how that turned out. You needed space to work, and I needed space to find myself in this school. And I think we still need that. But maybe we can have both. Like, be two distinct people with two distinct lives who *share* those lives, rather than this, like, inseparable couple?"

"HuntJor?" Hunter asked. "Jornter?"

"Ewwwww!" Jory laughed. "Please, no!"

"HUNTY?!"

"NO!"

They fell out laughing and embraced. The moment was

broken as Beckett burst into the Club Room and threw his fists into the air.

"SHE NAILED IT! SHE BOOKED IT! BAILEY GOT THE PART!" he shouted to the heavens. Reo, Aziz, and Sasha followed in behind him, laughing at their exuberant friend.

"And he's leaving out one other crucial detail," Reo said. "Beckett asked her OUT and she said YES!"

"WHAT?!" Jory gasped. "BECK! That's my man!"

"No offense, Beckett, but I didn't think you had it in you." Aziz smirked.

"Kinda like how we didn't know you liked THEATER GAMES, Aziz!" Beckett shot back. Aziz turned red with embarrassment.

"Let's please never, never speak of that again," he said.

"Look!" Sasha shouted. "We're all HANGING OUT AGAIN!"

It was indeed a great feeling to have all of the Backstagers together again in the Club Room like old times.

"And just in time," Timothy said as he descended the stairs and entered the room, followed by Jamie. "Hunter is going to need you all as he starts the trials this week."

"This week?" Hunter blurted. "Oh man, do I have to go back to the Arch Theater? Battle more crazy creatures?"

"Even scarier," Jamie said with a grin. "You have to run *Phantasm*."

"WHAT?" Hunter was gobsmacked.

"Starting tonight, all the way through closing, you'll be the stage manager," Timothy said. "Rehearsals, tech, opening night. It will require every skill in the Backstager arsenal. Think you're up to it?"

Hunter looked around the room at his friends, who met him with encouraging smiles and nods. He knew that with them, he could do anything.

"Yes, sir," he replied.

"Good, because we have to do some much-needed college visits! Graduation will be here any minute," Jamie said.

"Well, then, I'd better get to it!" Hunter said, springing up with newfound energy. "Backstagers, we ready to nail this rehearsal?"

Everyone cheered in agreement.

"Then let's move out!" Hunter said, and they started up the stairs.

Then there was an ominous knock at the Unsafe door.

Everyone stopped cold.

Eyes met eyes. Breathing slowed to a hush. Hunter put out a hand, signaling his team to stay put as he crept cautiously toward the door. He picked up a flashlight in case he was met with another shadowy specter on the other side. He took a deep breath. He opened the door.

A tall figure stood in shadow just beyond the threshold. It stepped into the light: a tall, very gray, very solemn-looking man of about fifty in plain jeans and a T-shirt. He carried a notebook in his hand and had a serious expression on his face.

"Mr. Rample!" Sasha cried as he bounded for the man and latched on to his leg, an affectionate hug. The man's stern expression softened a bit.

"Hi, Sasha," he said. "Hi, boys. Sounds like I missed some excitement."

It was the first time they had seen their old faculty advisor since he was fired over their disappearance during *Lease,* and there was so much to catch up on. Rample had gotten a job crewing at a professional regional theater and had traversed their backstage to get to the Genesius backstage and to the Club Room. So he would never be too far away in case they ran into any serious trouble again. Timothy had called him to fill him in about the business with the Arch Ghost, and Rample had decided he needed to come see them right away.

"There was a legend," he explained, "passed down from Backstager to Backstager from long before my time at Genesius. It told of a set of magic items that were the very tools that created theater everywhere. The tools that built the Arch Theater itself. I thought it was bogus until I stumbled upon one myself."

He tossed the notebook in his hands to Jory, who recognized it immediately. When they had been trapped in the backstage during *Lease*, Jory discovered this very notebook. Whatever he drew in it instantly became real. Jory had used it to draw an escape path, and once safely outside, he learned that it had belonged to Rample when he was a student at Genesius.

"That notebook caused such trouble when I was a student, I threw it off the Patchwork Catwalk and decided to never tell a soul about it. But then Jory found it anyway. Like it wanted to be found. And now, it seems another artifact, the Ghost Light, has appeared to you all."

"What do you think it means?" Aziz asked.

"I haven't the foggiest," Rample replied. "But given the speed at which you have been discovering them after all this time hidden, it seems as if the backstage is presenting the Genesius Backstagers with these items."

He stood and peered at the Unsafe door.

"The Designer's Notebook. The Ghost Light. The God Mic. The Prop Box. The Carpenter's Belt. The Show Bible. The Master Switch. These are the items I was told about as a kid. I have to think the backstage chose you all to find them for a reason. I think you all ought to go in search of what that reason is."

Jory, Hunter, Beckett, Aziz, Sasha, Timothy, Jamie, and Reo looked at one another. After all they had been through, it sounded like an incredible challenge.

It also sounded like an incredible adventure.

ACKNOWLEDGMENTS

I would like to thank Maggie Lehrman, Andrew Smith, and everyone at Abrams Books for leading me to the incredible world of the Backstagers, and James Tynion IV, Rian Sygh, and everyone at BOOM! Comics for their generosity in letting me play in that world.

ANDY MIENTUS is an actor, singer, and songwriter who is best known for his roles in *Spring Awakening*, *Wicked*, *Les Misérables*, *Smash*, and *The Flash*. He lives in New York City.

RIAN SYGH is a comic artist and cocreator of the award-winning Backstagers comics. He lives in Glendale, California.

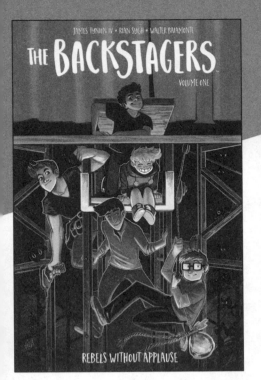 

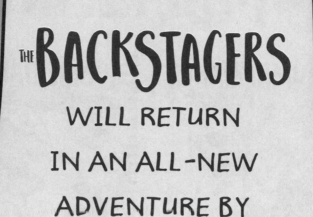

THE BACKSTAGERS

WILL RETURN
IN AN ALL-NEW
ADVENTURE BY
ANDY MIENTUS
COMING IN 2019!

CHECK OUT ANOTHER GREAT SERIES OF NOVELS BASED ON COMICS—

LUMBERJANES